P9-ARF-123

"You are due to receive your monthly allowance tomorrow."

Although he had not bothered to identify himself, there was no mistakng the deep, commanding tones of Leiandros's voice.

It was a voice that haunted her dreams, erotic dreams that woke her in the middle of the night, sweating and shaking.

"I won't be sanctioning that deposit, or any other, until you come to Greece." No explanation, just an ultimatum.

"The Greek Tycoon's Ultimatum is a compelling, sensual story. A romance you won't forget."
—bestselling author Lori Foster

GREEK TYCOONS

**They're the men who have everything—
except a bride...**

Wealth, power, charm—
what else could a handsome tycoon need?
In THE GREEK TYCOONS miniseries you
have already met some gorgeous Greek
multimillionaires who are in need of wives.

Now it's the turn of talented
Presents® author Lucy Monroe,
with her sensual and compelling romance
The Greek Tycoon's Ultimatum

This tycoon has met his match, and he's decided
he *has* to have her...*whatever* that takes!

Coming next moth:
The Greek Tycoon's Wife
by Kim Lawrence
#2360

Lucy Monroe

THE GREEK TYCOON'S ULTIMATUM

GREEK
TYCOONS

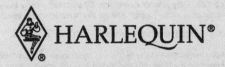

HARLEQUIN®

TORONTO • NEW YORK • LONDON
AMSTERDAM • PARIS • SYDNEY • HAMBURG
STOCKHOLM • ATHENS • TOKYO • MILAN • MADRID
PRAGUE • WARSAW • BUDAPEST • AUCKLAND

If you purchased this book without a cover you should be aware
that this book is stolen property. It was reported as "unsold and
destroyed" to the publisher, and neither the author nor the
publisher has received any payment for this "stripped book."

To my mother, Shirley Ann... The beauty of your
character and strength of your spirit in the face of
adversity is a constant source of inspiration for me.
Thank you for believing in my dream.

ISBN 0-373-12353-1

THE GREEK TYCOON'S ULTIMATUM

First North American Publication 2003.

Copyright © 2003 by Lucy Monroe.

All rights reserved. Except for use in any review, the reproduction or
utilization of this work in whole or in part in any form by any electronic,
mechanical or other means, now known or hereafter invented, including
xerography, photocopying and recording, or in any information storage
or retrieval system, is forbidden without the written permission of the
publisher, Harlequin Enterprises Limited, 225 Duncan Mill Road, .
Don Mills, Ontario, Canada M3B 3K9.

All characters in this book have no existence outside the imagination of
the author and have no relation whatsoever to anyone bearing the same
name or names. They are not even distantly inspired by any individual
known or unknown to the author, and all incidents are pure invention.

This edition published by arrangement with Harlequin Books S.A.

® and TM are trademarks of the publisher. Trademarks indicated with
® are registered in the United States Patent and Trademark Office, the
Canadian Trade Marks Office and in other countries.

Visit us at www.eHarlequin.com

Printed in U.S.A.

CHAPTER ONE

"THE coldhearted bitch."

Flinching as the words flew venomously from her sister-in-law's lips, Savannah Marie Kiriakis forced her gaze to remain fixed on the emerald-green grass in front of her.

The traditional Greek Orthodox graveside service was over and everyone had paid their final respects, everyone but her. Poised on the edge of the grave, a single white rose in her hand, she tried coming to terms with this—the final end to her marriage.

Relief warred with guilt inside her, forcing out the pain of Iona's verbal attack.

Relief that her own torment was over. No one would ever again threaten to take her children. And guilt that this should be her reaction to the death of another human being, particularly Dion—a man she had married in good faith and youthful stupidity six years ago.

"What right has she to be here?" Iona continued when her first insult was not only ignored by Savannah, but also by the other mourners.

Dion's younger sister had a flair for the dramatic.

Unbidden, Savannah's gaze sought the reaction of Leiandros Kiriakis to his cousin's outburst. His dark eyes were not set on Iona, but focused on Savannah with a look of such contempt if she'd been a weaker person,

5

she would have been tempted to jump into the grave with her dead husband.

She could not turn away, though her heart and emotions were screaming inside for her to do just that. Leiandros's contempt might be justified, but it hurt in a way that Dion's frequent infidelities and bouts of violent temper had not.

The smell of fresh earth mixed with the floral offerings covering the now closed casket assailed her nostrils and she managed to shift her gaze to her husband's grave.

"I'm sorry," she whispered soundlessly before dropping the rose she carried onto the casket and stepping back.

"A touching gesture, if an empty one." More words meant to wound, but these delivered directly to her with the sharp precision of a stiletto aimed at her heart.

It took every bit of Savannah's inner fortitude to turn and face Leiandros after the way he had looked at her a moment ago. "Is it an empty gesture for a wife to say her final goodbye?" she asked as she lifted her head to make eye contact.

And wished she hadn't. Eyes so dark, they were almost black, blazed with a scorn she knew she had earned, but nevertheless grieved. Of all the Kiriakis clan, this man was the only one with legitimate reason to despise her. Because he had firsthand knowledge of the fact she had not loved Dion, not passionately and with her whole heart as a man like her husband had needed to be loved.

"Yes empty. You said goodbye to Dion three years ago."

She shook her head in instinctive denial. Leiandros was mistaken. She would never have risked saying goodbye to Dion before fleeing Greece with her two small daughters in tow. Her only hope of escape had been to board the international flight for America before Dion realized she was gone.

By the time he had tracked her down, she had filed for a legal separation, thus preventing him from spiriting their children from the country. She had also filed a restraining order, citing her healing bruises and cracked ribs as evidence that she was not safe in Dion's company.

The Kiriakis clan knew nothing of this. Even Leiandros, head of the Kiriakis Empire and thus the family, was ignorant of the reasons for the final break in Dion and Savannah's marriage.

Leiandros's sculpted face hardened. "That's right. You never did say a final goodbye. You wouldn't give Dion his freedom and you wouldn't live with him. You were the kind of wife nightmares are made of."

Each word pierced her heart and her sense of self as a woman, but she refused to bow in shame under the weight of his ugly judgments. "I would have given Dion a divorce at any time over the last three years." He had been the one to threaten to take their daughters if she made good on her intention to file for permanent dissolution of their marriage.

Leiandros's face tightened with derision and she felt the familiar pain his scorn caused. His opinion of her had been cast in stone the night they met.

She'd been nervous attending a party given by a man she didn't know, a man Dion had raved about and stressed she had to impress in order to be accepted into the Kiriakis family. If that pressure had not been enough to make her tremble with anxiety, the fact that Dion had abandoned her in a crowd of strangers speaking a language she did not understand was.

Attempting to be unobtrusive, she hovered near a wall by the door to the terrace, away from the other guests.

"Kalispera. Pos se lene? Me lene Leiandros," A deep, male voice speaking in Greek penetrated her isolation.

She looked up to see the most devastatingly attractive man she'd ever encountered. His lazy smile all but stole her breath right out of her chest. She stared at him, mesmerized by a rush of inexplicable feelings toward him, unhindered by societal conventions or even unfamiliarity.

Feeling horribly guilty for such a reaction to a man who was not her husband, she blushed and dropped her gaze. Using the only Greek phrase she knew, she told him she could not understand his language. *"Then katalaveno."*

He placed a finger under her chin and forced her head up so she had no choice but to look in his eyes. His smile had turned vaguely predatory. "Dance with me," he said in perfect English.

She was shaking her head, trying to force her frozen vocal chords to utter the word *no* even as he put a possessive arm around her waist and pulled her out onto the terrace. He then drew her into his arms, his hold anything but conventional. She struggled while their bodies swayed to the seductive chords of the Greek music.

He pressed her closer. "Relax. I'm not going to eat you."

"But I shouldn't be dancing with you," she told him.

His hold grew even more possessive. "Why? Are you here with a boyfriend?"

"No, but—"

Demanding lips drowned her explanation that she was with her husband, not a boyfriend. Her struggles to get free increased, but the heat of his body and the feel of his hands caressing her back and her nape were already seducing her good intentions.

And to her everlasting shame she felt her body melt in helpless response. The kiss drew emotions from her Dion had never tapped into. She wanted it to go on forever, but even under the influence of a wholly alien passion, she knew she had to break away from the seduction of his lips.

The hand on her back moved to her front and cupped her breast as if he had every right to do so. The fact that he was touching her so intimately was not nearly so appalling as her body's reaction to it. Her breasts seemed to swell within the confines of her lacy bra while their tips grew hard and aching. She'd never felt this way with Dion.

The thought was enough to send her tearing from Leiandros, her sense of honor in tatters while her body actually vibrated with the need to be back in his arms. "I'm married," she gasped.

His eyes flared with the light of battle and she stood paralyzed for a solid minute, their gazes locked, their breathing erratic.

"Leiandros. I see you've met my wife."

And Leiandros, whose body was turned away from Dion so her husband could not see his expression had glared at her with a hate filled condemnation that had not diminished in six years.

"Do not fool yourself into believing that since my cousin is not here to defend himself, your behavior can be dismissed with lies."

Leiandros's voice brought her back to the present, to a woman no longer capable of any kind of response to a man. For a moment she grieved the memory of those awesome feelings she had not experienced since and knew she would never experience again. Dion had seen to that.

Leiandros's six-foot-four-inch frame towered over her own five feet, eight inches, making her feel small and vulnerable to his masculinity and the anger exuding off of him. She took an involuntary step backward and finding refuge in silence, she merely inclined her head before turning in order to leave.

"Do not walk away from me, Savannah. You won't find me as easy to manage as my cousin."

The implied threat in his tone halted her, but she did not turn around. "I do not need to manage you, *Leiandros Kiriakis*. After today, all necessity for communication between myself and your family will be at an end." Her voice came out in an unfamiliar husky drawl when she had meant to sound firm.

"In that, you are mistaken, Savannah." His ominous tone sent shivers skating along her nerve endings.

She whirled to face him, taking in the stunning lines of his masculine features, the way the sun glinted off his jet-black hair and the aura of power surrounding him even as she tried to read the expression in his enigmatic gaze.

"What do you mean?" Had Dion betrayed her in the end?

Leiandros's sensual lips thinned. "That is something we will have to discuss at a later date. My wife's graveside service begins in a few minutes. Be content with the knowledge that as sole trustee for your daughters' inheritance, you and I must of necessity talk occasionally."

Pain assailed her—a sympathetic pain for the grief this strong and arrogant man must be feeling at the death of his wife in the same car accident as his cousin.

"I'm sorry. I won't keep you."

His eyes narrowed. "Aren't you coming?"

"I have no place there."

"Iona thought you had no place here, yet you came."

Because of the phone call. She never would have come if Dion had not made that call the night before his accident.

"Regardless of what the Kiriakis clan would like to be true, I married Dion. I owed my presence here to his memory." Both the memory of the Dion who had courted her and the man who had called that one last time.

"Then do you not owe me your attendance at Petra's service as a member of my family?"

"Why in the world would you want me there?" she asked, unable to hide her complete bewilderment.

"You claim your place in my family. It is time you paid the dues accompanied by that status."

Humorless laughter fought to break free of the constriction in her throat. *Paid her dues?* Hadn't she done that for six long years? Hadn't she paid dearly for the privilege of wearing the Kiriakis name?

Leiandros watched emotions chase across Savannah's usually expressionless face. She hadn't been that way the first time they met. Then, she had seemed achingly vulnerable and sweet. So sweet she allowed another man to kiss her, to touch her while married to his cousin, he reminded himself.

Although she avoided eye contact with him on the few occasions they met after that, she'd still had an appealing vibrancy and beauty which made him understand why Dion stayed with her even after she had shown herself unworthy of her husband's respect and love. At least for the first year, but the one time Leiandros had seen her the second year she lived in Athens, she had changed beyond recognition.

Her green eyes had dulled to the point of lifelessness. Had guilt over her lovers done that? Her demeanor had completely lacked emotion—except when she looked at her daughter. Then a love Leiandros had envied—and hated himself for doing so—had suffused her face and brought life back to her green eyes. No wonder Dion ran wild with his friends. His wife had reserved all her emotion for the daughter she bore as the result of a liaison with one of her lovers.

Leiandros had chided Dion for showing so little interest in fatherhood after Eva's birth. Dion had cried when he told Leiandros that his wife had claimed the baby was not his. If Leiandros had ever doubted

Savannah's culpability in their shared kiss the night they met, he doubted no longer.

Remembering that encounter, his body tensed with anger. "Perhaps you are right. You have no place at my wife's funeral. One display of false grief within our family is enough."

Her eyes widened with what he could have sworn was fear before she took yet another step away from him. "I'm sorry Petra died, Leiandros."

The apparent sincerity in her soft voice almost touched him, but he refused to be taken in by her act a second time. She was no more the vulnerable innocent than he was a gullible fool. "I think you will be, Savannah."

"What do you mean?" she asked, her voice quavering in a way that annoyed him while she brushed a lock of wheat-colored hair away from her face.

What did she think he was going to do? Hit her? The thought was so ridiculous, he dismissed it out of hand. She had reason to be concerned, if not afraid. He did have plans for her, but they had to wait. "Never mind. I have to go."

She nodded. "Goodbye, Leiandros."

He inclined his head, refusing to utter a farewell he did not mean. After he expressed his respect for Petra with a year of mourning, Savannah would be seeing him again.

Then she would be made to pay for all that she had cost his family...all she had cost *him*.

CHAPTER TWO

SAVANNAH could hear the happy chatter of her daughters
playing in their bedroom as she settled into the creaking
desk chair in the small, cluttered study of her home in
Atlanta, Georgia.

She stared at the letter from Leiandros Kiriakis, feeling as if it were a black moccasin ready to strike. In it
he *requested* her presence in Greece for a discussion
regarding her financial future. Worse, he had demanded
Eva and Nyssa's presence as well.

He would be freezing Savannah's monthly allowance
until such a discussion occurred.

Panic shivered along her consciousness.

After the trial of attending Dion's funeral a year ago,
she had promised herself she would never have to see
anyone Kiriakis again. Okay, if not never, then at least
for a very long time.

The girls would have to be introduced to their Greek
family someday, but not before they were old enough to
deal with the emotional upheaval and possible rejection
of doing so. In other words, not until they were confident, mature adults.

She wished. She knew that wasn't realistic. Not after
the revelations Dion had made in that final phone call,
but she *had* intended to put the trip off for a while. Like
until she had a secure job and her Aunt Beatrice no
longer needed her.

Her mouth firming with purpose, she decided Leiandros would have to have his discussion with her over the phone. There was no earthly reason for her to fly all the way to Greece merely to talk about money.

Savannah's confidence in Leiandros's reasonability was severely tested ten minutes later when his secretary informed her he would not take Savannah's call.

"When would you like to fly out, Mrs. Kiriakis?" the efficient voice at the other end of the line enquired.

"I don't wish to fly out at all," Savannah replied, her southern drawl more pronounced than usual, the only indicator the conversation was upsetting her. "Please inform your boss that I would prefer to have this conversation by telephone and will await a call at his convenience."

She rang off, her hands shaking, her body going into fight or flight mode at the very thought of confronting Leiandros Kiriakis again in the flesh.

The phone rang ten minutes later.

Expecting Leiandros's secretary, Savannah picked up the receiver. "Hello?"

"You are due to receive your monthly allowance tomorrow." Although he had not bothered to identify himself, there was no mistaking the deep, commanding tones of Leiandros's voice.

It was a voice that haunted her dreams, erotic dreams that woke her in the middle of the night sweating and shaking. She could control her conscious mind, stifling all thoughts of the powerful, arrogant businessman, but her subconscious had a will of its own. And the dreams did nothing but torment her, as she knew without question she would never again experience those feelings outside the subconscious realm.

"Hello, Leiandros."

He didn't bother to return the greeting. "I won't be sanctioning that deposit, or any other until you come to Greece." No explanation, just an ultimatum.

The exorbitant prices Brenthaven charged for her aunt's care and the expense of attending university had prevented Savannah from accumulating more than a few weeks of living expenses in her savings. She needed the deposit to make her monthly payment to Brenthaven, not to mention to buy mundane items like food and gas.

"Surely any discussion we need to engage in can be handled via the phone."

"No." Again, no explanation. No compromise.

She rubbed her eyes, glad that he could not see the gesture that betrayed both physical weariness and emotional weakness. "Leiandros—"

"Contact my secretary for travel arrangements."

The phone clicked quietly in her ear and she pulled it away to stare at it. He'd hung up on her. She said a word that should never pass a lady's lips and slammed the phone back into its cradle. Shocked rigid by her own unaccustomed display of temper, she stood motionless for almost a full minute before spinning on her heel to leave the now stifling study.

She'd reached the door and opened it when the phone rang again. This time it wasn't Leiandros or his secretary. It was the doctor in charge of Aunt Beatrice.

Savannah's beloved aunt had had another stroke.

Savannah tucked her daughters into bed, telling them their favorite rendition of the Cinderella tale for their bedtime story before ensconcing herself in the study to make the dreaded call to Leiandros.

She pulled up her household budget spreadsheet on the computer and ran the numbers one more time. Nothing had miraculously changed. She *needed* the monthly allowance. Even if she could manage to land a full-time job the very next day, starting wages in spite of a degree in business were not going to be enough to cover their household expenses and the increased cost of Aunt Beatrice's medical care.

Savannah picked up the phone and dialed Leiandros's office.

His secretary answered on the first ring. The conversation was short. Savannah agreed to fly out the following week, but she refused to bring her daughters. The secretary hung up after promising to call back within the hour with an itinerary.

Savannah was making herself a cup of hot tea in the kitchen when the phone rang only minutes later.

A sense of impending doom sent goose bumps rushing down her arms and up the backs of her thighs. She just knew the secretary wasn't calling back with travel plans already.

After taking a steadying breath, she picked up the phone. "Yes, Leiandros?"

If she'd hoped to disconcert him, she was disappointed as there wasn't even a second's pause before he started talking.

"Eva and Nyssa must accompany you."

"No."

"Why not?" he demanded, his Greek accent pronounced.

Because the thought of taking her daughters back to Greece terrified her. "Eva has almost two weeks left of school."

"Then come in two weeks."

"I prefer to come now." She needed the money now, not in two weeks. "Besides, I see no reason to disrupt the girls' schedule for what will amount to an exhausting, but short trip."

"Not even to introduce them to their grandparents?"

Fear put a metallic taste in her mouth. "Their grandparents want nothing to do with them. Helena made that clear when Eva was born."

She'd taken one look at Savannah's blue-eyed and blond-haired baby and decreed the child could not possibly be a Kiriakis. Eva's eyes had darkened to green by the time she was a year old and her baby fine hair had been replaced by a thick mane of mahogany waves by the time she was four.

It was too bad Helena had refused point-blank to even come to see Nyssa. Savannah's youngest had been born with the black hair and velvet brown eyes of her father.

Unmistakably a Kiriakis.

"People change. Their son is gone. Is it so strange Helena and Sandros should wish to know his offspring?"

Savannah sucked in much needed oxygen and marshaled her thoughts. "Do they now acknowledge Eva and Nyssa as Dion's?"

"They will when they meet them."

No doubt. Both her daughters had enough physical characteristics of the Kiriakis clan that once seen their parentage could not be challenged, but that did not mean she was ready to introduce them to their family in Greece.

"How can you be so sure?" she asked, wondering how he knew of her daughters' physical resemblance to their relatives.

"I have seen pictures. There can be no question Eva and Nyssa are Kiriakises." The words sounded like an accusation.

"Dion's pictures, you mean?"

She'd sent him frequent updates on the girls' progress along with photos, hoping that one day he would show some inclination to acknowledge them. She'd felt her own lack of family and mourned her inability to know her own father and did not want the same grief visited on her daughters.

"Yes. I supervised the disposal of his effects from his Athens apartment." Again Leiandros's voice was laced with censure, as if she should have done the job herself.

After three years of separation and living independent lives on two different continents, she hadn't even considered such a thing. "I see."

"Do you?" he asked, his voice silky with unnamed menace and that awful sense of dread washed over her again.

"Have Helena and Sandros expressed a desire to meet them?"

"I have decided the time has come."

And as the head of the Kiriakis clan, he expected the rest of the family to go along with whatever decision he made.

"No."

"How can you be so selfish?" Condemnation weighted each word with bruising force.

"Selfish?" she asked, feeling anger roiling in her stomach, making it churn. "You call it selfish for a mother to wish to protect her children from the rejection of people that are supposed to love them, people that should have loved them since birth, but decided for their own obscure reasons not to?"

She knew she wasn't being entirely fair. For six years, Savannah had believed Dion's family had hated her because she was not the suitable Greek bride they had chosen for him to wed and therefore rejected her children. His phone call the night before he died effectively obliterated that theory.

Along with other stunning revelations, her dear husband had admitted that he'd been poisoning their minds with his insane jealousy, accusing her of infidelity, from almost the very start of their marriage. Helena and Sandros had what they believed to be legitimate reasons to question the parentage of Savannah's daughters, but that didn't make her any more willing to expose Eva and Nyssa to possible rejection and pain.

"Sandros and Helena will accept the girls with open arms."

"Who do you think you are. God?"

Funny, she could actually sense the fury sizzling through the phone lines. He was not used to being questioned. He'd been in charge of the huge Kiriakis financial empire since his father's unexpected death when Leiandros was twenty. At thirty-two, his arrogance and sense of personal power were as ingrained and natural to him as making his next million.

"Do not be blasphemous. It is unbecoming in a woman."

She almost laughed out loud at how stilted he sounded, like someone's maiden aunt giving lessons in etiquette. "I'm not trying to be offensive," she replied, "I simply want to protect my daughters' best interests."

"If you expect those interests to include further financial support from the Kiriakis family, you will bring them to Greece."

Savannah tried to draw in a breath, but it seemed to get stuck somewhere between her windpipe and her lungs. The edges of her vision turned black and she wondered with a sense of detachment if she were going to faint. Leiandros didn't know it, but he was forcing her to choose between the elderly aunt who had raised her and the safety of her daughters' emotions along with her own sanity.

It was her second worse nightmare. The first had already happened. She'd married Dion Kiriakis.

"Savannah!"

Someone was shouting in her ear. Her hand instinctively tightened on the phone and the room came slowly back into focus.

"Leiandros?" Was that thready voice hers?

How pathetic she must sound to the self-assured man on the other end of the line, but then she doubted anyone had ever forced him to do anything he did not want to.

"Are you all right?"

"No," she admitted. The last of her emotional reserves seemed to have dissipated with his overt threat.

"Savannah, I'm not going to let anyone hurt Eva and Nyssa." His voice reverberated against her ear with conviction and assurance.

But would he let them hurt her? "How can you prevent it?"

"You will have to trust me."

"I don't trust people named Kiriakis." Her words came in the flat monotone she couldn't seem to shake.

"You don't have a choice."

Leiandros hung up the phone, satisfied.

The opening gambit had gone to him. It would only be a matter of time before he captured her.

Savannah and her daughters would be flying to Greece the day after Eva's school let out for the summer. Savannah had agreed only after extracting a promise from him not to instigate any meeting between Eva, Nyssa and their grandparents before she had an opportunity to speak to Helena and Sandros.

How could she now show such concern for her daughters' emotional well-being when her lies about their parentage had denied them the love of their family since birth?

No doubt, her arguments were an attempt at manipulation. Perhaps she intended to try to use the girls as bargaining chips for a larger allowance. While her current stipend was substantial, it would hardly support the designer clad, jet setting lifestyle she had experienced while living with Dion.

He put through a call to his secretary. "Arrange for my jet to land in Atlanta to transport Savannah Kiriakis and her children to Athens two weeks from today."

He cut the connection after giving his secretary other necessary details.

Savannah had balked at flying on his jet, but after he

told her the plane had a bedroom the girls could use to sleep in comfort, she had agreed. If she'd remained insistent he would have given in to her. The first step in his plan was the most important: getting Savannah and the girls to Greece.

Savannah had to be on the chessboard in order to engage her in the game.

He would not allow an ocean and two continents to prevent him from exacting full payment from her for all that she had cost his family, all that she had cost *him*.

Savannah had committed the gravest of all sins against his family, that of withholding her children, using lies and manipulation to cheat Dion out of his fatherhood and Helena and Sandros out of their rightful role as doting grandparents.

That would end in two weeks time.

When he had first met Savannah, he had been drawn to her apparent innocence, to the impression of untouched sensuality she had exuded. So drawn he had kissed her without knowing her name or anything else about her.

She had struggled at first, but within seconds had gone up in flames. Her response had been more exciting than any other sexual experience he'd ever had. Then, she'd yanked herself from his arms and told him she was married. His first, primitive instinct had been to tell her she had married the wrong man. And then her husband had arrived. *His cousin.*

Leiandros's body still remembered the feel of hers. His mouth still hungered for her taste. His sex still ached for the release denied him that night. No matter how he tried to forget the forbidden desire for his cousin's wife, she was always there, in his dreams, in his mind.

Even knowing she was a scheming, heartless witch, he wanted her. Now, he would have her. She would replace what he had lost and in the process, he would sate his body's urge to possess her.

CHAPTER THREE

SAVANNAH carried a sleeping Nyssa toward customs, following Leiandros's personal flight attendant who led an equally worn-out, but barely awake, Eva by the hand. Exhaustion dragged at Savannah and she looked forward to a shower with almost religious fervor.

She could have taken one on the plane, but had not wanted to wake Eva and Nyssa any sooner than she had to. Wound up by the excitement of flying in an airplane, they had not made proper use of the plane's bedroom until an hour before landing.

When they reached customs, she was given VIP treatment and rushed through, an example of Leiandros's power and far reaching influence. It increased the sense of a trap closing around her she'd had since stepping onto his private jet.

As she stepped into the main terminal, she forced her weary eyes to focus on the scene around her. The new airport was all modern glass and streamlined walkways, but still incredibly crowded. She sighed and shifted her grip on Nyssa. Her arms felt like two strands of pasta cooked al dente.

Even as her gaze swept the crowded terminal, she felt the fine hairs on the back of her neck stand on end. Turning her head slightly to the right, she met the dark, inscrutable gaze of Leiandros Kiriakis himself and she stopped. Not voluntarily. Her legs simply quit working.

She hadn't expected to see him until the next day.

The flight attendant paused beside her, forcing the stream of air passengers to break and flow around them. "Mrs. Kiriakis? Is something wrong?"

Savannah could not make her lips form words. Her entire being was caught up in this first sight of Leiandros Kiriakis in a year. His black hair had been cut to lie close to the sculpted lines of his head. His sensual lips set in a grim line, his eyes betrayed nothing. He made no move to come toward them, but seemed content to wait, towering with unconscious arrogance above the sea of humanity that welled around him.

Taking a tighter hold on her sleeping daughter, she stepped forward only to bump into another passenger. "Excuse me. I'm sorry."

The woman she'd bumped ignored Savannah and scurried away toward the luggage carousel.

A large man who looked like a Greek Sumo wrestler barreled into her from behind. Stumbling, she feared she would lose her hold on Nyssa when two strong hands gripped her upper arms and steadied her. How had he gotten to her so quickly?

"You're dead on your feet, Savannah. Let me take the child." Leiandros moved one hand from her arm to Nyssa's back.

Without conscious volition, Savannah yanked herself and her daughter out of touching distance from Leiandros. "No. I can carry her, but thank you," she tacked on belatedly.

His eyes narrowed.

"Mama..." Eva's tentative interruption saved Savannah from whatever Leiandros had planned to say.

Savannah turned her attention gratefully to her daughter. "Yes, sweet pea?"

"I'm tired. May I go to bed now?"

"It will be a little while before we reach your bed, but you can sleep in the car. The seats are big enough for a little girl like you to treat them like a bed," Leiandros said.

"I'm five," Eva announced.

His mouth quirked. "If you are five, you must be Eva. I am Leiandros Kiriakis."

Eva's head tipped back and she measured him with a drowsy but direct look. "Kiriakis is my name, too."

He squatted down until his face was almost level with that of Savannah's serious little daughter. He matched Eva's grave expression. His mouth curved into a devastating smile. "So it is. That is because we are family."

Eva tugged her hand away from the flight attendant's and sidled next to Savannah, taking a grip on the loose fabric of her crushed silk trousers. "Is he my family, Mama?"

Leiandros's eyes blasted Savannah with sulfuric fury briefly as he straightened to stand at his full impressive six feet four inches. He seemed to be daring her to deny the link to her daughter, which she had no intention of doing.

She hadn't been the one to deny her daughters' family ties. "Yes, darling, your father was his cousin."

"Does he look like my father?" Eva asked.

Leiandros speared Savannah with another look of censure.

"You've seen pictures, what do you think?"

Savannah replied, letting her daughter draw her own conclusions.

She felt Eva's head shift against her thigh as the little girl nodded her head. "But maybe he's bigger."

Eva put her hand on Nyssa's small leg dangling over Savannah's arm. "This is Nyssa. She's four."

He acknowledged the introduction with a devastating smile.

"Now that we are acquainted, it is time we left. Felix will take care of the luggage," he said, indicating a short, stocky man standing several paces away near another very muscular man, only a couple of inches shorter than Leiandros.

Leiandros led them outside and Savannah blessed the lightweight nature of her crushed silk pantsuit when the hot Greek air blasted her as they stepped out of the air-conditioned environs of the recently completed airport. While the heat wasn't so very different from Georgia, the sun's impact felt stronger.

As they approached a black limousine with darkly tinted windows, the chauffeur opened the back door while another man stood sentry on the driver's side. He and the man with Felix were no doubt part of Leiandros's security team.

Savannah motioned Eva to climb in first. She did, taking Leiandros at his word and making herself comfortable for sleep on the far side of the seat, leaving enough space for Savannah to lay Nyssa's dozing form down as well. Another wave of exhaustion rolled over her and Savannah wished she could join Nyssa in her peaceful slumber. Within fifteen minutes of leaving the airport, Eva had done so.

"Sleep if you wish. I will not be offended," Leiandros offered. "The trip is a long one from the airport."

Savannah swallowed a yawn. "I didn't think it was that far from the city."

"It is not, but there is road construction." He shrugged. "It will take us at least two hours to reach the villa."

She'd been relaxing against the seat, preparing to take him up on his advice to pass the time sleeping when he made that comment. She sat straight up and twisted her body until she could look him full in the face.

"What villa? I thought we were staying at a hotel."

"You are family. You will stay with family."

There was that word again, but Savannah had had enough experience her first time around in Greece with the dutiful ties of the Kiriakis family not to trust them.

"You promised me the girls would not have to see their grandparents until we discussed it," she accused him in a fierce whisper, not wanting to wake her daughters to hear this particular argument. "I insist you take us to a hotel."

"No."

"No? No! How dare you do this? You promised." She settled back against the seat with her arms crossed. "I knew I couldn't trust a Kiriakis."

That seemed to get him, because his hands curled into fists at his side and his face looked hewn from rock.

"You will not be staying with Helena and Sandros."

"You said we'd be staying with family, at the villa." As the words left her lips, an awful thought occurred to her. "You want us to stay at *your* villa on Evia Island? *With you?*"

His brows rose in sardonic challenge. "My mother is also staying at the villa. She will be sufficient chaperone."

"*Chaperone?* I don't need a chaperone. I need privacy. I need to stay in a hotel."

"Relax, Savannah. There is no reason to shout about it. With two active children, you will find the villa much more comfortable than a hotel, I promise you."

In that respect, she had no doubt he was right, but it wasn't her daughters she was worried about at the moment. It was herself. She shuddered inwardly at the prospect of sharing living space with Leiandros.

"I suppose you still keep an apartment in Athens and spend most of your time there," she said hopefully.

"Yes."

She couldn't quite stifle her sigh of relief.

"Of course, I've arranged to work from the villa for the next few days so I can spend time with *my family*."

Savannah's throat went tight in reaction to the threat in his voice, despite the innocence of the sentiments expressed.

"How long did you plan our visit to last?" It was something he'd refused to discuss on the phone.

If she'd been in her right mind, instead of riddled with worry over her aunt, Savannah would have forced the issue.

Leiandros looked at her as if trying to read her mind. "We'll discuss that tomorrow."

"I'd rather discuss it now." She kept her expression purposefully blank.

"Very well." He shrugged again, his face wearing a strangely watchful air. "Permanently."

"*Permanently?*"

The grim line of his mouth went even more taut. "Yes. You've spent enough time running from your family. It's time you came home, Savannah."

Home? She wanted to shriek at him and pound her fists, but even with rage coursing through her veins like molten lava, she held onto her temper. She'd learned that lesson much too well to forget it, even with the current provocation.

She'd lost her control once with a Kiriakis male and opened herself to physical reprisal from her husband. She still had nightmares about her last meeting with Dion, the feeling of bruising male fists landing against her unprotected flesh.

"America is my home," she said, spacing the words evenly, keeping her voice flat.

"It was your home before you married a Kiriakis, yes. But now Greece is your home, specifically my villa."

"Your villa? You expect me to live in your villa permanently?" She was in a waking nightmare.

He reached out and opened the minifridge, pulling out a bottle of water, handing it to her before taking one for himself. "Yes."

She stared at the cold plastic bottle in her hand, wondering for a second how it had gotten there. "I can't."

He didn't bother to argue with her. In fact, he didn't answer her at all. Instead, he pulled a buzzing cell phone from his pocket and answered it.

*   *   *

Savannah slowly regained consciousness, uncertain what had wakened her, and shifted in the cocooned warmth of her make shift bed. She burrowed her face into the pillow, which felt strangely hard against her cheek. Unsated exhaustion tugged at her, tempting her back into an unconscious state.

Her bed moved and the blanket pressed against her back in a soft caress. "Wake up *pethi mou*, we have almost arrived."

Her eyes flew open. For the space of several seconds she couldn't even breathe. The blanket caressing her back was in fact a large, male hand and her firm pillow, a muscular chest. Frozen into immobility by shock, she further discovered that her arms were wrapped tightly around his torso.

The subtle fragrance of fresh, clean male and expensive aftershave teased her senses. Familiar and yet unknown. She blinked, trying to focus, but her vision was clouded by crisp white silk and her mind could not quite come to grips with the first intimacy shared with a man in well over four years.

And not just any man.

She was wrapped up like an early Christmas present in the arms of Leiandros Kiriakis.

Reality so closely matched the dreams that had tormented her subconscious for seven long years that she spent several precious seconds trying to determine if she were still asleep.

"Eva, how come Mama is hugging that man?" Nyssa's voice unlocked Savannah's frozen limbs.

She was definitely awake. Her daughters had never played a role in the dreams she had had about Leiandros. Yanking her arms from their snug nest in his suit coat, she launched herself from Leiandros with such a violent movement she bounced against the opposite door and nearly fell off the seat.

He reached out to steady her and she recoiled violently from the possible touch. "I'm fine," she all but snarled, her usual polite reserve a forgotten ideal.

"He's our family," Eva said, as if that explained everything. She had that much in common with her uncle.

Savannah couldn't help but wonder if he had thought the familial claim justified the intimacy of their position as well.

"Mama?" Nyssa asked, her brown Kiriakis eyes wide with curiosity.

Savannah settled herself more firmly on the large limousine seat. Not caring what Leiandros thought of the action, she scooted as close to the door as she could get without sitting on the armrest. "Yes, sugar?"

"Why did you hug the big man?"

"I wasn't hugging him." She turned and glared at Leiandros. This situation was all his fault. "I was asleep."

"Oh." Nyssa turned her interested gaze to Leiandros and stared at him in silence for several seconds before turning back to her mother. "Were you sitting in his lap to sleep?"

The heat of embarrassment crawled over Savannah's skin like ants on a picnic blanket. She couldn't look at Leiandros. She had no idea how she'd ended up sleeping with her body plastered against his and feared finding out she had been the instigator.

The last thing she remembered was letting her head rest against the back of the seat. She'd closed her eyes in weariness as she tired of waiting for him to finish the latest of his numerous business calls on the cell.

She'd obviously fallen asleep. That she could understand. She'd been nearly comatose from exhaustion before the plane had landed. The last two weeks had been peppered with sleepless nights and emotionally draining days visiting her aunt.

Even so, she found it difficult to believe she'd allowed herself to get that close to a man, asleep or not. Her subconscious mind might crave Leiandros Kiriakis, but her conscious mind rejected even the hint of intimacy with any man.

The evidence, however, was irrefutable. Her skin still tingled from where she had touched him.

Before she got a chance to form a reply to Nyssa's question that wouldn't betray the rawness of her nerves, her daughter smiled at Leiandros. "Sometimes I sit on my mama's lap for sleeping, but she says I'm getting too heavy. Isn't she too big for your lap?"

Savannah wanted to groan out loud at her daughter's logic. Nyssa's nap had clearly been long enough to rejuvenate her mind as well as her spirits. Savannah wished she had been so lucky. Her mind felt too sluggish to deal with the current situation. Unbelievably, her traitorous body craved return to the warm, muscular resting place of Leiandros's chest.

"I'd say she's just right." His low, sensual tone caressed Savannah's insides, making them tighten and interrupting her chaotic thoughts.

Awareness of his masculinity bombarded her. Along with something else, something elemental that left her feeling hot and strangely edgy. *Impossible.* She had spent the last four years believing she would never again experience sexual desire and here she was as jittery as a mare being bred for the first time. Wanting it, but terrified at the same time.

"Where are we?" she asked in a desperate bid to change the direction her thoughts were taking.

"Very near Villa Kalosorisma. We have just crossed the bridge to Evia Island." His eyes told her he knew exactly why she'd asked the question and found the knowledge amusing.

The car slid to a halt and seconds later, the door next to Savannah opened. The chauffeur helped first Eva, then Nyssa from the car. By the time Savannah swung her legs around to climb out, Leiandros had exited from the other side and come around to take her hand in his.

He pulled her from the sleek chauffeured car, the heat of his hand branding her as intimately as if he'd kissed her. She tried to ignore the sensation and swiftly stepped away from him.

The girls stood a few yards away, staring at the villa's front with identical expressions of surprised awe. Savannah identified with the feeling.

She had never been to Villa Kalosorisma. Dion had kept her separated from the rest of his family as much as possible, even his parents and sister. He'd told her at the time it was his way of protecting her from their disapproval until they came to accept the marriage. She now knew differently. He'd been afraid of having his ugly lies about her morality revealed. She still cringed at what a gullible idiot she had been then.

The pristine whiteness of the villa's stucco exterior dazzled her eyes, contrasting beautifully with the red tile roof. Three levels of terraces outlined by arches fronted the mansion. Surrounded by immaculate gardens and green trees, through which she could see glimpses of sparkling blue sea, Villa Kalosorisma simply took her breath away.

"It's a real pretty hotel," Nyssa announced.

"It's not a hotel," Savannah felt impelled to say.

"This is my home." Leiandros had come to stand behind Savannah without her realizing it.

She once again stepped away, impatient to put distance between herself and his disturbing presence. She'd almost grown accustomed to the anxiety a man's nearness caused in her, but that anxiety mixed with unmistakable sexual awareness was a cocktail mix guaranteed to corrupt her sanity.

"I thought we were staying in a hotel, Mama." Eva said.

"In Greece family is everything. It would be considered a grave insult were I not to offer my home to you all and equally offensive if your mama refused to accept it." Leiandros's words seemed laced with warning and Savannah turned her head to see him more clearly.

Was he trying to intimidate her and if so, why? She'd already agreed to stay at his villa and in fact felt a small measure of gratitude that she hadn't been forced to play this scene with Helena and Sandros. She would have refused any invitation extended by them regardless of the offense taken.

The very thought of being forced to accept her in-law's hospitality was enough to make her feel slightly nauseous.

"Our house is lots smaller because we've just got a

mommy and me and Eva. You must have an awful lot of kids. You're house is like Cinderella's castle.'' Typically, Nyssa had spoken again while Eva silently watched the adults, letting her serious green gaze flicker between them and the big white villa.

Bitterness and pain reflected briefly in his dark chocolate eyes. ''I have no children.''

''Oh. Don't you like kids?'' Nyssa asked before Savannah thought to caution her daughter to silence.

This time the pain was more pronounced and even slipped into his voice as he answered. ''I like children very much.''

Had he and Petra planned to have them right away? It must have been a horrible shock to lose her so soon after marriage. Leiandros and Petra had only been married about a year when Dion crashed his car with Petra in it, killing them both instantly. Knowing it was ridiculous, Savannah still felt guilty by association. It had been her estranged husband responsible for the crash.

Eva stepped forward and laid her little hand on Leiandros's forearm. ''It's okay. Someday, you'll have some. Mama says you've got to believe in your dreams for them to come true.''

He squatted down in front of Eva and reached out to brush her cheek. ''Thank you, *pethi mou*. You and your sister staying at the villa will be like having children of my own.''

In a wholly uncharacteristic move, Eva let her small fingers trail down Leiandros's face to his chin, her green eyes full of both compassion and a wistfulness that surprised Savannah. ''I'll play checkers with you if you like. Daddies do that with their little girls sometimes.''

"You can help Mom tuck us in at night, too," Nyssa added, not willing to be outdone by her sister.

Savannah watched the entire scene with a sense of unreality intensified by her tiredness. Her daughters had spent very little time around men, which usually made even the more gregarious Nyssa timid with them. And yet, here was Savannah's extremely cautious eldest daughter reaching out to touch Leiandros.

Even more shocking than her daughter's response to Leiandros were *his* words. Did he truly want her and the girls to move to Greece to fill a void that had opened in his life since his young wife's death?

She'd never considered Leiandros Kiriakis vulnerable in any way. The man spent his time running a multibillion dollar corporation. He couldn't seriously need the company of two small girls to complete his life.

Savannah curled her hands around the oversized woven bag she carried. It felt like a link to sanity, its casual American styling a reminder of the life she'd made for herself and her daughters. A life far removed from that of privileged wealth exemplified by Villa Kalosorisma.

A life she and her daughters *would* return to.

CHAPTER FOUR

LEIANDROS sipped his neat whiskey and waited for Savannah to join him in the fireside reception room before dinner.

The villa, built by his grandfather, boasted two large reception rooms as well as two formal dining rooms, one of which his father had turned into a study after losing the smaller area dedicated to that purpose to a TV viewing room at his wife's request. There was also a breakfast nook, eight bedrooms with en suites and full staff quarters on the ground level.

In other words, his home had plenty of space for Savannah to find the privacy she said she craved, but such privacy would not extend to her avoiding his company. That was not part of his plan. Tonight, he intended to make it clear to her he would be an intrinsic part of her life from now on.

He was so hungry for her, he had been unable to resist the growing temptation to pull her into his arms after she fell asleep. He'd watched her for several miles of travel before giving into the urge to pull her into his arms.

He had not held her, even in an embrace of greeting, since the hot kiss they had shared the night they met. He could not risk his own body's reaction. Touching her then had been wrong. She'd belonged to another man.

Dion had died and now Savannah belonged to Leiandros, even if she did not yet realize it.

Her body had known it. She'd curled around him like a lover of longstanding and his physical reaction had been predictable if surprisingly swift. He'd wanted to touch her, to remove her soft silk blouse and see the breasts pressed so tantalizingly against his chest, but even Greek tycoons had their sense of honor, he thought cynically.

When he touched Savannah, she would be awake and wanting it as much as he did.

As she had wanted his kiss seven years ago.

He took another sip of his whiskey as she appeared in the arched doorway. She'd changed into a knee length sheath in emerald green raw silk and pulled the multi-colored, golden brown strands of her hair into an elegant twist on the back of her head. Her only jewelry was a necklace of hammered silver medallions and matching earrings.

It was a lovely look, but hardly the designer labeled couture he'd expected from her based on the monthly allowance she received. Nyssa had also said their house was small.

Was that the unrealistic view of a child, or had she been stating a fact? If Nyssa had spoken the truth, what did Savannah spend the ten thousand dollars a month she received from the Kiriakis coffers on?

Savannah hovered in the doorway, wanting to flee. The girls had been fed and put to bed an hour ago. They had invited Leiandros to help tuck them in, but he'd had to take an international call and had promised to do so the following night.

Savannah hadn't minded one bit. She found his presence distinctly disturbing.

"Come in, Savannah. I'm not going to eat you."

She forced a slight smile to her lips and a light tone to her voice. "Of course not. Billionaire Greek tycoons have too much discernment to eat houseguests, even reluctant ones."

His black brow raised in cynical amusement. "What would you like to drink?"

"Something nonalcoholic. I have no head for spirits and in my current state of jet lag, I'd probably pass out after a sip of your most innocuous sherry." And she needed her wits.

He turned toward the drink trolley, his gorgeous body graceful in movement and yet exuding power. He poured her a tall glass of chilled water over ice, adding a twist of lime to it.

She accepted the drink, making sure their fingers did not touch and then took a step back. "Isn't your mother joining us for dinner?"

He moved forward, closing the small gap she had created. "She's visiting friends. She'll be home in a couple of days."

"So much for her suitability as a chaperone," Savannah muttered under her breath.

He laughed softly. "You said you didn't need one. Have you changed your mind, Savannah?"

His deep, masculine voice vibrated through her, causing her insides to tighten in a frightening way and she felt her cheeks heat at the reaction and the import of his words. She took a long, cooling sip of water. "Mr. Kiriakis, we need to talk."

"Leiandros. Not Mr. Kiriakis. Not *Kyrios* Kiriakis. Leiandros. We are family. You will not address me so formally again."

Her intention had been to create distance between them mentally, if not physically, but clearly she'd managed to annoy him as well. She gritted her teeth. It just wasn't worth making an issue over. "Leiandros then. This idea you have of the girls and I making a permanent home in Greece is unfeasible at the present time to say the least."

His eyes narrowed while he indicated with a gesture of his hand she should sit down on one of the almond leather sofas on either side of the fireplace. "Why?"

"I have obligations, commitments, back home that I cannot dismiss." She chose a seat on the far end of the sofa located on the other side of the room from him.

His smile was predatory as he followed her and took a seat on the same sofa, his body turned toward hers. "What kind of commitments?" he asked with obvious suspicion.

She felt his presence like a physical force and she had to concentrate to answer his question. "The usual kind." She crossed her legs at the ankle while taking another sip of her drink. "Relationships. Work. My commitment to Eva and Nyssa's well being."

"You do not have a job."

She acknowledged the truth of his statement with a brief nod. "But I do need to have one if I'm ever to be free of my dependence on the monthly allowance." Surely he must see that.

"If independence is so important to you, why have you made no move to get a job in the last four years?" he demanded, skepticism lacing every word.

Her free hand curled into a fist and she felt her face tighten with anger before she made herself relax and her face go blank of emotion. "I've spent the last four years going to university. I now have a degree in business and plan to use it to support myself and my daughters.''

He looked absolutely stunned and she felt satisfaction at the reaction.

"Did you bring your diploma with you?" he asked.

Had he lost his mind? "Why would I bring it with me?"

"So I can verify you are telling me the truth."

Unaccustomed and unwelcome anger filled her. "Your arrogance is astounding. Why should I have to prove myself to you? My degree is immaterial to the discussion at hand."

"Which is what?" he asked, his voice laced with sensual innuendo.

She swallowed, trying to ignore the way her heart reacted to that particular honeyed tone. "We are discussing my need to return home. Soon. I'll stay long enough for the girls to meet their grandparents if my discussion with them proves satisfactory, but then I'm going home and there's not a blessed thing you can do about it."

"You'd be surprised at what I have to say about it."

She gritted her teeth. How could she feel threatened by him and attracted to him at the same time? "You can *say* what you like, but I'm still going."

"If you really are interested in gaining your independence from the monthly allowance I provide, why have you come to Greece at all? You didn't want to come, but you agreed when I refused to pay it."

That was not a question she was willing to answer. "You don't provide our allowance. It comes from the girls' trust." She set her now empty glass down on a small table.

"I haven't touched Eva and Nyssa's trust in the past year."

"But…" She let her words trail off, nonplussed. *He'd* been paying their allowance for the past year? The knowledge made her feel strange, as if he had intruded into her life in an intimate way without her being aware of it.

"There are no buts. I have supported you for the past year and if you wish me to continue to do so, certain conditions must be met."

She'd had it up to her neck with conditions from Dion. She wasn't going to go that route with Leiandros. "I don't want to be supported. I'm perfectly willing to get a job."

"Then why have you come to Greece?" he asked again, his disbelief palpable.

"I need our allowance for another few months, until I'm on my feet financially."

"Do you honestly believe you'll be able to get a job starting out at ten thousand dollars a month?" He made it sound like she was the world's biggest idiot.

"No. Of course not, but I won't need that much money to live on in a few months." Her heart contracted with a spasm of grief at the thought of why she wouldn't need so much money.

The doctors did not expect her aunt to live to the end of the year. Without the monthly payments to Brenthaven, she and the girls could easily live on her income.

"Again I ask why?"

"You're like a dog with his favorite bone."

He shrugged. "So, answer me and I'll quit asking."

She met his gaze, hers level and as impassive as she could make it. "The answer is none of your business."

He didn't like that. His dark eyes flared with affronted pride. "Since I am paying your allowance I think it is."

"But I didn't *know* that."

"You do now."

Desperation edged her voice. "It can't change anything. I still need the money right now. Perhaps, we could make it a loan and once I've gotten a job I could pay you back in monthly installments."

She'd been forced to pull her entire savings to pay the increased costs of the round-the-clock care her aunt needed since the last stroke, but another payment would be due in only a couple of weeks.

Brenthaven had a strict policy requiring advanced payment for services. If she did not keep up-to-date, they would transfer Aunt Beatrice to the nearest state nursing home. They might regret the need to do so, but would do it nonetheless as she had discovered four years ago when she had separated from Dion without a financial support agreement.

Felix announced dinner before Leiandros responded to her suggestion of a loan.

Savannah tried to do justice to the excellent dinner Felix's wife had prepared, but jet lag and the stress of trying to spar verbally with Leiandros had stolen her appetite. Not to mention the strange vibrations that shivered through her whenever she let her eyes meet Leiandros's. Even her favorite moussaka tasted like sawdust in her mouth.

Leiandros pushed his empty plate aside while eyeing her nearly full one. "You should have taken a tray in your room. You're too tired to enjoy a full course dinner.''

''We needed to talk without interruption.'' Or witnesses. She did not want her daughters to know that Leiandros sought to have the Kiriakis women back in Greece permanently.

''So, talk. You can begin by telling me what significant change you anticipate in your circumstances that will make it possible for you to go from living on ten thousand dollars a month to a fraction of that.''

She didn't like the speculative look in his eyes. Nor did she have any intention of telling him what he wanted to know. If he found out about Aunt Beatrice, he would have the same stick to beat her with Dion had used so effectively.

''My financial needs are my concern. If you won't lend me the money, I'll take out a mortgage on my house.'' There was no reason to let him know that option was an iffy one at best without a proven source of income.

She had to hope Leiandros's pride would not allow a Kiriakis to go to a bank for what the family had been providing up to date.

He said nothing as the housekeeper removed their dinner plates and put small crystal bowls of fresh fruit and cream in front of them.

She smiled at Savannah. ''I think you'll eat this, yes?''

Savannah returned her smile. ''Yes. It looks very refreshing.''

Silence reigned as she and Leiandros ate their dessert.

When they were finished he told the housekeeper they would take their coffee on the terrace and led Savannah outside. The view from the back terrace was every bit as spectacular as it was from the bedroom windows. The sea glistened gold and red and even the pool shimmered with exotic color in the sun's setting light. She gave an involuntary sigh of appreciation.

"There is nothing more beautiful." Leiandros pulled a chair out for her from the white wrought-iron patio set.

She sat down, her gaze shifting from the vibrant sunset to the tall, dark man at her side. "Sunrise in a grove of Magnolia bushes isn't such a paltry sight, either."

His teeth flashed in the waning light before he took the chair nearest her own, putting his back to the spectacular Heavenly display and focusing his entire attention on her. "One day I may have to see that."

The thought of Leiandros in Georgia was enough to unsettle her nerves and send her stomach into cartwheels. "I can't imagine you finding sufficient business incentive to make the journey," was all she said.

Felix's wife arrived with a tray bearing two demitasse cups filled with the traditional aromatic, spiced Greek coffee. She also turned on the outside lights, illuminating the pool and the garden surrounding it, before returning to the house.

Several lighted pathways led into the orchards and olive grove surrounding the house. Savannah longed to explore their quiet solitude, but she had to remain with Leiandros and impress upon him her seriousness about returning home and her need for the monthly allowance to be deposited immediately into her account.

"Kiriakis International does not dictate every aspect of my life." The timbre of his voice and dark chocolate depths of his eyes spoke a sensual message that both frightened and excited her.

"I find that difficult to believe considering the amount of time you have always spent working." She took a sip of her coffee, allowing her senses to savor the unique flavor. She had missed this little luxury back in Georgia.

"And yet I found time to marry."

The thought of Leiandros married to another woman made her feel raw inside, mitigating the effectiveness of her usually stringent guard on her tongue. "To a traditional Greek girl who undoubtedly never questioned her role in your life."

His scowl said he did not appreciate her view. "Is that why you abandoned my cousin? Wasn't he willing to cater to your need to be the center of his universe?"

Savannah felt her emotions and thoughts close down as they always did at any mention of her disastrous marriage. "I had no desire to be the center of Dion's life."

She had in fact wished fervently that he had been less focused on her, particularly when that focus came in the guise of irrational jealousy and his desire to impregnate her with his child. His *male* child.

"I imagine that is true. Dion's obsessive love must have been an unexpected cramp in your pursuit of *friendships* outside of your marriage."

The way he sneered the word friendships left her in no doubt about just what nature he believed those relationships had taken. Savannah had learned from Dion that denial was useless and defending herself only left her open to further accusations and insults. So, she didn't even bother to try.

She simply said, "Obsessive is a very good name for the feelings Dion had for me."

"The poor fool loved you." Leiandros made it sound

as if only an idiot would have such tender feelings for his wife.

"I suppose you were too much in control of your emotions to make the same mistake with Petra."

His jaw tightened. "I cared for my wife. She had a life most women envied, but you are right. I never subjugated myself to her the way Dion did with you."

Subjugated? Dion? Leiandros's view of her marriage would be laughable if the truth didn't hurt so much. "I prefer not to discuss my marriage."

"So sensitive. Are you trying to convince me that the subject is painful for you, or merely distasteful?"

Once again, she took refuge in her coffee. She needed time to collect her emotions before speaking. When she did, she was proud of the even tenor of her voice. "Dion and I were estranged for years prior to his death. I consider my marriage a part of my past that has no place in my present or future."

"You forget your daughters. They are a product of that marriage that preclude you dismissing it completely from your life." It was as if he was challenging her to deny Eva and Nyssa were Dion's daughters.

"Surely after seeing my daughters, you cannot doubt that Dion was their father."

"I do not deny it, no. It is you that have withheld the girls from their Greek relatives practically since birth." The accusation in his voice was unmistakable.

Anger, usually suppressed, burned through her reserve. "I was not the one who questioned their Kiriakis heritage. If you wish to lay blame for that, look to your cousin and his unreasonable jealousies. It was because of them that his mother pronounced Eva a cuckoo in the family's nest and refused to acknowledge her. She and

Sandros never even made the effort to see Nyssa. Not once in the six months before I left Greece or the years since.''

''How convenient. You can dismiss your role in your daughters' estrangement from their family because Dion no longer lives to give lie to your claims of innocence.''

The pig. Of course he doubted her. After all, his male cousin would never have lied to him. Dion's jealous delusions were taken as gospel by his staunchly loyal family. She could admire that loyalty, but she didn't have to become a victim to it. She'd fought too hard to make something of herself and her life to allow Leiandros to tear away at her carefully constructed foundation with his cruel words.

Discussion over the monthly allowance would have to wait.

She stood up. ''I'm tired. I believe I'll go to bed.''

''So regal when running away. What's the matter, Savannah? Does the truth distress you so much?''

Her hands clenched at her sides while she willed the anger inside her to remain hidden. ''I have discovered that Kiriakises are not interested in truth so much as their own delusions. I have no hope of changing yours so I refuse to try, but I also refuse to sit and listen to a character assassination based on those delusions. Good night.''

She turned to walk away.

Suddenly he was there beside her, his long, masculine fingers wrapped securely around her upper arm. ''Oh, no. You aren't walking away from me so easily. Dion may have let you dismiss him like a tame lapdog, but be warned I am a wolf in comparison.''

Her heart had started to accelerate at the first touch of

his fingers and her breath shortened to panicky pants as the threat in his voice washed over her.

"Please, let me go." She didn't sound regal any longer. Her voice had come out weak and way too soft.

"Not yet. There is something I need to do first."

Was he going to hit her? She refused to cower, but she also hesitated to use the self-defense techniques she'd learned to dislodge his grip. She did not wish to hurt him and her heart denied vehemently any notion he would physically hurt her. Which led her to ask herself where her heart had gotten such an idea? The answer terrified her more than the memory of Dion's rage. On some level she did not understand, she trusted Leiandros physically in a way she did not trust any other man.

For the moment, she stood immobile in his arms. "What?"

"I neglected to kiss you in greeting at the airport. It is time I rectified that omission, don't you think?"

His words paralyzed her. She and Leiandros had not shared so much as a handshake since their disastrous first meeting. Of course he would not have greeted her in the traditional Greek manner at the airport.

"There is no omission to correct."

He propelled her around to face him and placed his free hand under her chin. "Ah, but there is."

She would have argued further, but he lowered his head and touched one of her cheeks briefly with his warm, firm lips. "Welcome home, Savannah."

She waited for the panic, which typically accompanied such close proximity to a male, but as in the limo, her body did not react with its usual desire to flee. Her mind *was* panicking however because as he kissed her other cheek, she had an inexcusable urge to turn her face so instead of the platonic salute to her cheek, she would receive a kiss full on the mouth. She fought the impulse, managing to remain immobile in his hold.

He didn't step away after kissing her second cheek, but remained close to her for several, tense, silent seconds.

"Don't you wish to return my greeting?"

She did. The desire was such a new experience after years of experiencing nothing but fear and distrust in the company of a man that she acted on it without thought. He released her chin and she kissed him on first his left cheek, then his right.

She could taste the clean saltiness of his skin and smell his distinctive cologne. She wanted to kiss him again, but she didn't. She waited to see what he would do next.

He didn't leave her in suspense long. He made an inarticulate sound deep in his throat and then covered her still tingling mouth with his own.

Her eyes slid shut and fireworks exploded in and around her. One second she was standing a safe distance from his virile male body and the next she was plastered against him with her hands locked fiercely behind his neck.

She opened her mouth for his invading tongue without a second's hesitation and eagerly entered the erotic duel he initiated. It was as if her body could not resist the feast of his touch after the famine she had imposed on it for so many years. It felt so good to be close to him.

He tasted like ambrosia to her passion starved mouth and she lost all conscious volition to control her actions. She operated on instinct and desire, both of which urged her to hold nothing back from this volatile kiss.

His large hands moved down her back to cup her buttocks. He squeezed and an involuntary moan of pleasure exploded from her mouth into his. He used his hold on her to lift her and press the apex of her thighs against his throbbing hardness.

She couldn't help arching into him any more than she could wrench her mouth from his marauding one.

It felt too delightful. It was even more devastating than the kiss they had shared the night they met because she had no voice of conscience telling her that she was a married woman who had no business feeling passion with a man not her husband.

Dion was gone and her body knew it.

She wanted Leiandros with a strength that overwhelmed her good sense, her fear of a man's nearness, even her sense of self-preservation that she had spent four years honing. Her nipples hardened into rigid peaks that strained against the soft lace of her light bra and she could feel moisture gathering between her legs in anticipation of the kiss's outcome.

Leiandros kneaded her bottom with his hands, helping her achieve maximum friction between his hardened maleness and her aching femininity, while sucking on her tongue and playing erotic biting games with her lips.

She rocked harder against him, overwhelmed by the sense of bliss his body gave to hers.

Pleasure began washing over her in waves and she whimpered, frightened of these new and overpowering feelings. He made approving sounds as his mouth continued to devour hers, but he lifted one hand from her bottom to caress the aching rigidity of her right nipple. He pinched it gently through the layers of raw silk and lace and something exploded inside of her.

She went rigid while her body convulsed in his hold, her cry of fear mingled with pleasure getting swallowed by his hot, hungry mouth. She shook and shook before her body went boneless. If he had not held her, she would have melted into a dazed puddle at his feet.

So that was what it felt like. She'd never known pleasure so glorious, nor sensations so intense. She could not prevent herself from wondering what it would be like with his body joined to hers. Could it possibly be better?

His arms wrapped around her, pressing her body close in an embrace that comforted her devastated emotions, while he drew his mouth away to kiss her eyelids, her cheeks, her nose, and even her chin.

She started to cry, quiet sobs so alien to her that they were almost as frightening as the mind-blowing pleasure.

He kissed the wetness from her cheeks, acting as if the tears were his due. "There can be no doubt our marriage bed will be a satisfying one."

CHAPTER FIVE

SAVANNAH stared in disbelief at Leiandros. Had he just said they were going to get married?

She shook her head, but her mind refused to clear.

Without warning, he swung her high against his chest and carried her into the house and up the stairs to her room where he deposited her on the side of her bed. Her mind vaguely registered that he wasn't even breathing hard.

He cupped her nape and pressed his lips briefly and gently against hers, which clung without volition. "Good night. We'll discuss plans for the future tomorrow."

It was a measure of her bemusement that instead of disabusing him of any ideas of a shared future together, she merely nodded and watched quietly as he left the room, closing the door behind him. It took ten full minutes of silent contemplation of that same closed door before the enormity of what she had done hit her.

She had let Leiandros kiss her and touch her intimately on a well lit terrace where anyone could have seen them. Worse, her body had betrayed her by finding the ultimate pleasure at his touch. She hadn't even considered fighting him off or denying him access to her femininity. If he had undressed her and offered to share her bed, she would have let him.

She didn't think she could ever look Leiandros in the

eye again. How on earth was she supposed to discuss money and her now even more necessary return to America with him?

An involuntary smile curved her lips because her shock and dismay were tinged with a sense of elation she could not deny. The essence of her womanhood, the part of her she had believed destroyed by her husband's violence the last time they saw each other, was alive and well. She'd reclaimed her femininity and she'd done it with Leiandros Kiriakis.

She pushed herself into a standing position beside the bed, somewhat surprised when she remained vertical. She should take a shower. Yes, that's what she should do. Wash away the evidence of her desire and the effect of Leiandros's kisses. She walked over to the white wicker dresser and removed her jewelry, laying it on the glass top.

Unzipping her dress with fingers that still trembled, she moved toward the closet. She slid the dress from her body, sucking in a breath of shocked air at the way her nipples and thighs responded to the movement of the raw silk. Pressing the dress to her heated cheeks, she could smell her own perfume, but the faint fragrance of Leiandros's sexy cologne lingered on the fabric as well.

She stood there inhaling the evocative scent until she realized what she was doing and hastily hung the dress up. If she had thought removing her dress had been erotic, it was nothing compared to the reaction she had to taking off her underclothes. By the time she had tossed them in the round wicker clothes hamper, she recognized that a hot shower was the last thing her sexually awakened body could handle.

She slipped into a sleeveless white cotton nightdress with embroidery on the three button yoke. She'd always considered the nightgown rather innocent, but tonight it reminded her of a virgin waiting to be ravished on her wedding night.

Groaning at her wayward thoughts, she climbed between the Jasmine scented polished cotton sheets of her bed. Wasn't Jasmine supposed to be some kind of aphrodisiac? She certainly didn't need any more stimulation. Maybe she could ask the housekeeper for some plain sheets that smelled like good old-fashioned fabric softener tomorrow.

She snuggled into her pillow, sure she'd never get to sleep after the shattering events of the evening, but her eyes were heavy and her body felt replete in a way it never had before.

Her last drowsy thought was that Leiandros was more effective than a sleeping pill.

Leaving Savannah alone in her bedroom had been one of the more difficult tasks Leiandros had set for himself, perhaps even the most difficult task to date. He wasn't going to make love to her when she was suffering from exhaustion and jet lag. He would not allow her the out that she hadn't been in her right mind when she finally gave her body to him.

Besides, there was something he needed to do.

Picking up the phone, he dialed a well-used number. It answered on the second ring. "Raven here."

"Leiandros Kiriakis. I need some information."

"Person or company?"

"Person. Savannah Kiriakis of Atlanta, Georgia."

"Isn't she your cousin's widow?"

Leiandros leaned against the edge of the desk. "Yes."

"I see."

"I doubt it."

"What do you want to know?"

"Everything. I want to know who she sees. If there's a man in her life. She claims she's recently graduated from university. I want verification of the claim. But most of all, I want to know about her financial situation. She's been getting ten thousand American dollars a month in allowance, but she doesn't dress like it. According to her daughter, they live in a modest house. I want to know where that money is going and why she thinks she won't need it a few months from now."

"Is that all?" Raven asked with more than a little sarcasm tingeing his distinct British accent. "And I suppose you want the information yesterday."

"Yes." Leiandros didn't explain why. He didn't have to. He paid Raven well to find information and rarely shared his motive for wanting it with the private investigator.

"Lucky for you it's the afternoon in the States. My contacts there shouldn't have any problem tracking down this information for you."

"Good."

"Do you want it in a phone call or fax when I get it?"

"Fax. There could be pictures." He was thinking of the possibility that Savannah was seeing a man.

He'd taken that for granted considering how she had behaved while still married to Dion, but after the way she'd exploded like a roman candle in his arms tonight, he had to wonder if her social life had been as active as he'd imagined.

"Right." Raven hung up.

Leiandros put the phone down as well before going to his own room to take a cold shower and go over the details of his plan. It had to be airtight. After what he had shared with Savannah on the terrace, he was even more determined to bind her to him in marriage and establish her in his bed.

He would never let go of her again.

"Watch me, Mama. Watch!" Nyssa's demand brought Savannah's gaze from the aquamarine depths of the sea to the clear glistening water of the swimming pool.

Nyssa stood poised on the edge of the deep end, while Cassia, the nanny Leiandros had hired to help with the children, swam a few feet away. Leiandros had apparently been quite serious about her and the girls making their home with him, to the extent he had hired a permanent, full-time nanny. When the housekeeper had introduced Cassia to Savannah at breakfast, Savannah's first reaction had been to refuse any help with her daughters. However, the young Greek girl's obvious eagerness to please had stilled the words on Savannah's tongue.

As soon as she saw that Savannah was indeed watching, Nyssa launched herself toward Cassia, landing in the water with a huge splash. Savannah clapped her appreciation as her daughter went down, touched bottom and bobbed back to the surface before swimming to the side of the pool and climbing out to do it again.

Swinging her gaze to Eva, Savannah smiled in encouragement at her older daughter. Eva, who had been waiting quietly for her mother to notice she was on the verge of doing her own trick, did a standing dive in the water at the shallow end and brought her legs together straight up in the air. She proceeded to spread them in a V and then bring them together once more.

"Cool," Nyssa said, "I want to do a handstand, too."

Eva came up for air.

"That was wonderful," Savannah called.

"I agree."

The deeply masculine voice acted like a shot of adrenaline to Savannah's senses and she jerked in reaction. She could not make herself lift her eyes to meet his, certain she would see mocking disdain for her total loss of control the night before in the dark chocolate depths.

He came to stand behind her, so close she felt the electric charge zinging between them and did her best to ignore it, while reveling in the new experience of not wanting to back as far away from a man as possible.

"They're a couple of water babies," he said approvingly.

She inclined her head toward him, her gaze focused on the first level terrace near the house and realized her mistake almost immediately. But it was too late to block the memories the white wrought iron patio set invoked. She could feel her skin heating with embarrassment and something else. *Desire.*

"Yes. Eva and Nyssa have both always loved the water. They had swimming lessons when Nyssa turned two." She hoped the small quiver in her voice had not betrayed her mixed up emotions.

He picked up the paperback she'd brought outside, letting his hand skim her leg as he did it. "Savannah?"

She tensed, her thighs clenching against the feelings that even such a slight, careless touch could produce. She did not believe for one second the touch had been accidental. "Wh-what?"

What did he want with her book? He wasn't even looking at it, from what she could tell. She could be wrong because she still couldn't make herself meet his gaze.

"I do not like talking to the top of your head." He tapped the paperback against his palm.

Well she didn't like talking to him period. "Oh."

"Would it be so difficult to look at me?" The condescending humor in his voice chipped at her pride.

She mentally steeled herself to face the man whom she'd shared herself so intimately with without any sense of true intimacy between them and raised her head. Her mental steel felt more like melting aluminum. He looked even more devastating in his white polo and khaki linen trousers than he had in his suit. Every line of muscle was revealed by the knit fabric and cleverly cut linen.

Her fingers itched to trail over the defined muscles of his chest. She wished her sunglasses were mirrored, but though they were very dark, they were still revealing. Could he see the impact just looking at him had on her?

Why was she worried about her eyes? Her nipples would give her away any second. Already, they were growing tight and achy. She crossed her arms protectively over her chest, glad she'd done so when she could feel the tight points of her breasts drilling into her forearms. "What did you want?"

"To talk."

About last night? About her allowance? About her

staying in Greece or more alarmingly, about his shocking remark concerning marriage?

"This isn't a good time or place," she replied, indicating Cassia and the girls playing together in the pool.

"I agree the place is inappropriate. Interruptions will only make our discussion more difficult. But the time is, I think, ideal. Cassia can watch the girls and they all appear content to play in the pool for a bit longer."

"I don't want the girls overexposed to the sun," she said, desperate for an excuse to put off a confrontation between them.

"I'm sure Cassia is capable of taking them inside for showers and a snack at the appropriate time. She is a trained nanny."

"One you hired without my consent or input."

"Is there a problem with Cassia? If so, we can find an alternative nanny."

"I have a problem with you trying to dictate my life."

He laughed softly. "Are you coming?"

Savannah acknowledged defeat and her own cowardice at the same time. Leiandros wasn't going to forget her hedonistic pleasure in his arms the night before any more than she would. Putting off talking to him would only prolong the inevitable, not change it.

"All right." She stood up, putting the lounger between them. "Just let me talk to Cassia and then I'm all yours."

As the words left her mouth, she realized the connotation they could take and nearly bit her tongue.

Leiandros just smiled, *his* eyes hidden behind mirrored sunglasses. "You already are."

She felt like letting loose a string of very unladylike

expletives at his arrogance. She glowered at him, wishing glares really could singe their recipients.

"I'm not," she said, sounding like an angry six-year-old and not all that convincing.

His smile did not dim and he didn't bother to argue with her, which was a much more effective form of disagreement than words would have been.

She spun away, her foot hitting a patch of water on the tile that hadn't evaporated since Eva had come to stand next to her earlier. One foot went forward while the other remained sedentary and she felt herself falling backward toward the lounger, but once again like at the airport, Leiandros was there to catch her.

His big hands curved around her ribcage as he leaned over the lounger to hold her upright. "Careful, *yineka mou.*"

The endearment shocked her as much as the feel of his long fingers pressing against the underside of her unfettered breasts. She'd worn a loose India cotton summer dress cut straight and long and dyed in shades of brown so she could take advantage of the cooling affects of not wearing a bra. She regretted that decision deeply as his forefingers shifted slightly against her breasts and their tips went hard and pointed again in the space of two seconds.

Both the endearment and the action spoke of a possession she didn't want to acknowledge.

"Did you dress this way for me?" he asked in a quiet, sexy voice close to her ear.

"No," she denied quickly, too quickly. "It's hot. I'm not very big, so it's not usually a problem to go without…without…'' For the life of her, she could not say the word *bra* to him.

What did that make her? She'd behaved like a crazed wanton in his arms last night and today stumbled over a perfectly normal word like a blushing virgin. Did that make her sexually schizophrenic, she wondered wildly?

He allowed his palms to cup her intimately for just a second before sliding his hands back to their former, more respectable, position. ''I'd say you are just right.''

She gasped and darted a look at the pool. Cassia and the girls were playing a game in the shallow end, their backs to her and Leiandros.

''Don't do that.'' The words sounded breathless and wispy.

Leiandros not only seemed to have a hold over her body that frightened her, but he also decimated her control in a way that one else did. Even her daughters in a temperamental mood could not agitate her the way he did.

''But your body is so responsive to my touch. Any man would find that irresistible. I am no different.''

She wanted to hit him. She really did. Preferably with a brick bat. Responsive? Irresistible? He could at least have the decency to find her attractive, instead he was all over conceited about her response to him. She called him several choice names in her head before she felt calm enough to speak.

''Let me go. I can stand on my own now.''

Surprisingly he did.

She walked to the side of the pool and gave Cassia

instructions on what to do with the girls over the next hour or so, hoping Leiandros's big discussion would not take more time.

Leiandros led her into the study and closed the door behind them. "I've informed Felix we are not to be disturbed."

Savannah licked nervously at her bottom lip. "I see."

Great. Not only did he make her hard earned self-control disappear but he had her speaking in inanities as well.

"Sit down." He indicated a burgundy leather covered wing chair in front of the large polished mahogany executive desk at one end of the room.

She sat.

"Drink?" he asked, opening up a mini bar fridge cleverly disguised as one of the richly lustrous mahogany cabinets that made up the lower portion of the bookcases lining most of the room's interior walls.

"Yes, please. A wine spritzer."

"Since you do not usually drink alcohol, I have to assume you think you need a fortifier for our upcoming discussion." His sardonically raised eyebrow made a mockery of her carefully neutral expression.

He knew she was nervous, darn him. "I could have a mineral water just the same."

He ignored her, pouring a small amount of wine into a glass and then adding club soda to it. He handed her the glass with a faintly mocking expression. She immediately took a sip.

He poured himself chilled fruit juice and somehow she felt as if she'd made another mistake. His thinking wasn't going to be clouded by alcohol during this discussion. At least she'd eaten a substantial lunch only a little over an hour ago.

She waited in silence for him to open the dialogue. He would not intimidate her into asking questions that might give away her own inner anxieties. And if marriage was going to be discussed, she sure as heck wasn't going to be the one to bring up that disastrous subject.

He moved to lean against the desk in front of her chair, almost sitting on the edge. His legs were far too close to her own. Taking several sips of his fruit juice, he watched her with his damnably compelling eyes.

She took matching sips of her spritzer while forcing herself to meet his gaze, to show him she wasn't going to be cowed by his silence, though she doubted her green eyes were compelling so much as frightened. This situation would be so much easier if last night's proceedings had never happened.

Embarrassment played havoc with her need to remain cool, in control of herself and the situation.

When about half of his juice was gone, Leiandros spoke. "We can be married next Sunday. I've already seen to the legal formalities and booked a priest. Naturally we will be married in the chapel on the villa's grounds."

Her glass dropped to the Turkish carpet and though she noticed the spreading stain of white wine and club soda on the colorful rug, she did nothing to stop it. She couldn't. Her mind had gone numb. Leiandros Kiriakis had just said he wanted to marry her and this time she was sure she wasn't imagining it.

The thought was both tantalizing and overwhelmingly frightening. The fear she understood. The fear made sense. What woman who had suffered through the marriage she had had with his cousin would look forward to the prospect of marrying again? But the allure of the idea completely flummoxed her.

She couldn't seriously *want* to marry another Kiriakis. Could she? Did this mean she loved him? The thought made her feel ill. She had absolutely no illusions that such an emotion was motivating Leiandros. He did not respect her. He thought she'd had affairs while she was married. No way could he love her, but she didn't know what *was* motivating him, either.

She said the only thing she could say. "No."

He didn't look offended. In fact, he laughed. Not uproariously, not even with any real humor. His laugh sounded dark and if she were in a melodramatic frame of mind, she would think diabolical.

"I did not ask you a question. I told you of certain upcoming events." His voice was strangely gentle.

It sent shivers skittering the length of her spine and made all her fine body hairs raise in acknowledgment of true terror. He sounded so confident of her agreement.

She took several deep breaths focused on calming herself. "This is not the middle ages. You have to have my agreement for any marriage to take place and I'm not giving it."

His black eyebrow quirked. "You think not?"

"I know not."

"I believe you will change your mind when all the facts of the situation are made known to you."

"What facts?" she could not help asking.

"You are aware that Dion's will named me sole executor and trustee of his estate?"

"Yes." Did he think he could blackmail her with the money?

"Are you also aware that Dion named me Eva and Nyssa's guardian in the event of his death?"

"What do you mean? I'm their mother and sole guardian."

He bared his white teeth in a semblance of a smile. "In the States that is true, yes. But in Greece, I am their other guardian. You cannot take the girls out of the country without my consent. I assure you, I will keep much better track of you than my cousin. You will not sneak out in the middle of the night and spirit them back to America without my knowledge."

She had to breathe shallowly for several seconds to combat the nausea roiling in her stomach. She could actually feel the blood draining from her face. "You can't mean to keep my daughters from me."

He shook his head, his mouth grim. "No. I mean to marry you and keep you all in Greece. Together."

"I can't stay here." She thought of her aunt, stable for the moment, but with only months, perhaps weeks to live. "I need to return to Atlanta. I have responsibilities there."

"Responsibilities you will not be able to fulfill if you do not get an immediate influx of cash."

"No," she whispered. He couldn't know about Aunt Beatrice. "Why are you doing this to me? You can't want to marry me."

"You are wrong. I consider it a matter of justice."

"Justice?" For Dion?

"Because of you, I lost both my cousin and my wife."

"How… How do you make that out? I wasn't even in Greece when the accident happened."

His entire body tensed with rage that burned out of his eyes almost black with the emotion. "Exactly. You weren't here to be a proper wife. You stole his daughters. You stole his manhood. Dion went off the rails, looking for solace in parties and wild living. He took Petra with him."

She shook her head. "If Dion was so unstable, what was your wife doing with him?"

"They were friends. He was my cousin. His accident was caused because he had been drinking, trying to drown his sorrows that his latest request for you to bring his daughters to Greece had been rejected."

How could he believe such tripe? "You think Dion was a saint, don't you?" she asked with helpless despair.

"Not a saint, but a man who had been sorely mistreated by his wife." The accusation was there in his voice, in his eyes, in the way he leaned over her with intimidating fury.

Her hands trembled and she clasped them together tightly in her lap to stop the telltale sign. "I told him he could visit the girls. He didn't need to drown his sorrows."

"You expect me to believe this?"

"If you think I'm so hateful and dishonest why would you want to marry me?"

"You owe me."

"What? What do I owe you?"

"You owe the Kiriakis family your daughters to replace the loss of their father. You owe me a wife. You owe me a child."

"A child?" she asked faintly.

"Petra was four months pregnant with our son when she died."

Savannah shot clumsily to her feet, her body feeling sluggish from the shock of his words. "No."

"*Yes,*" he hissed. "You are going to marry me and give me a child to replace the son I lost."

Her skin felt cold and red lights danced in front of her eyes. "No."

"Yes." Implacable. Angry. Determined.

The world went black around the edges and she felt her muscles falter before a welcome dark oblivion claimed her.

CHAPTER SIX

"WAKE up, *moro mou*. Come on, Savannah. Come back to me."

The alluring voice pulled her to consciousness along with the sensation of cool wetness caressing her face and neck.

Her eyes fluttered open. She was lying on the burgundy leather sofa at the opposite end of the study from the desk. Leiandros sat next to her supine form, bathing her neck with a cold, damp cloth, his touch incredibly gentle.

She stared at him, bemused. Her mouth felt cottony. Her head felt light, like she'd had too much champagne. But she hadn't been drinking champagne. Had she? No. A wine spritzer. And she'd only drunk about half of it before…

Her stomach started to churn as memory came flooding back.

She went stiff and pushed Leiandros's hand away. "You blame me for your wife and baby's death." Just saying the words increased the sick feeling in her stomach.

He put the cloth down on a table, his expression enigmatic. "Apportioning blame is unimportant, now. Justice will be served when you marry me and become pregnant with my child."

She struggled to sit up and he helped her, the strange

71

gentleness she'd woken to still in evidence. He had managed to lift her without shifting his own position, so now the hard muscle of his thigh brushed against her legs trapped on the sofa next to him. She tried to edge away, but had nowhere to go. "I won't marry you, Leiandros. I won't let you use my body as a broodmare to prove your own masculinity."

She'd had enough of that with Dion.

Leiandros reached out and tucked a wisp of hair behind her ear, allowing his long, male fingers to caress the sensitive skin there before removing them. Her breath caught even as she jerked her head away.

He smiled. "I have no need to prove my masculinity, but I do desire children and you are going to give them to me."

Another wave of dizziness passed over her. *"No."*

"You have no choice," he said, reminding her of the threats he'd made before she was swallowed up in the black void.

"You're wrong," she said, refusing to give into the fear his words invoked. "You can force me to stay in Greece by holding my daughters hostage, but only until I convince the court to allow them to return to Atlanta. *You cannot force me to marry you.*"

She could only hope if he saw his goal of marriage and procuring Savannah as a baby incubator as unattainable, he would let her and the girls go home. He had never struck her as the kind of man to pine after lost causes. He would find another nice traditional girl, like Petra, marry her and give *her* his babies. Savannah ignored the unexpectedly unpleasant image of a faceless brunette pregnant with his child biting into her consciousness.

"I think I can." Leiandros laid his hand on her thigh in a gesture that was both intimate and intimidating. "Consider this, Savannah. You have no money, but that which I give you. No means to hire a reputable Greek lawyer to argue your case, no resources with which to fight for sole guardianship of Eva and Nyssa. And I will fight. You cannot doubt it."

The insidious seductiveness of his voice almost blinded her to the content of his words. "No. It's not worth it to you."

His masculine lips tilted in a mocking smile as he began moving one finger on her thigh in small geometric patterns. "Isn't it?"

She couldn't think. The feel of his hand on her, even through a layer of clothing brought forth the most electrifying sensations in her body. Her gaze moved from his unrevealing features to the sight of his hand on her thigh. She should stop him, but all she wanted to do was take that hand and place it where her flesh ached the most. What was happening to her?

Her body had been dead for four long years. How could it come alive for a man who threatened her peace and stability?

"Eva and Nyssa belong in Greece," he was saying and her scattered attention found its way back to his mouth.

She watched the lips move in paralyzing fascination, knowing she should be listening to the words, but too enthralled by glimpses of the interior of his mouth to focus on anything so mundane. Memories of how those warm depths tasted tormented her mind and titillated her body.

"Any case brought before a Greek judge will naturally be heavily swayed in my favor. In Greece, family is everything and I am not seeking to separate you from your daughters, merely to see them raised among their only known extended family."

Finally his words penetrated and she came crashing to the reality of the present with a thud even as his hand came dangerously close to the apex of her thighs. Her body galvanized into action and she grabbed his wrist. She tried to wrench it away, but he was as movable as a rock. At least, he stopped the disturbing little caresses.

She tried to school her features into a familiar blank mask, but felt cracks around the edges. "I'll sell my house to finance the fight," she bluffed with an edge of desperation.

"What about your aunt?" he asked, his voice silky with both threat and smug certainty. "By the time your house is sold, she will have been moved to a state nursing facility."

Everything inside her went still. He'd discovered the stick and now he meant to beat her with it. Defeat stared her in the face. "You're worse than Dion," she grated.

That seemed to startle him. His eyes narrowed. "What do you mean by that?"

She shook her head, unwilling to expose her deepest hurts for him to exploit to his own advantage. "How did you find out about Aunt Beatrice?"

"I made a call last night to a private investigator. I received his report this morning."

He'd had her investigated. Her entire body went stiff

until each individual muscle felt like a rubber band pulled to its limit. "What else did he tell you?"

"Many interesting things." He squeezed her thigh.

Using both hands this time, she jerked at his wrist again, and managed to slide his hand a couple of inches away from her most vulnerable flesh. "I don't want you touching me."

"Really?" Pitiless brown eyes mocked her. "You like it. A minute ago you were practically begging for more."

"I wasn't."

He laughed, the sound more ominous than amused. "You were." He leaned toward her, his hand once again moving inexorably closer to her femininity and even under two layers of fabric, she felt unprotected against his imminent assault. "Shall I prove it to you?"

She shook her head. "No. Don't." She was begging him and she didn't care. If he kissed her, she would be lost.

His mouth was only millimeters from hers, his warm breath caressing her lips while his masculine scent surrounded her. "Admit it."

She leaned back until her neck was stretched beyond comfort. "No." No defiance in that whispered little word, just despairing appeal.

He smiled as if she already had and pulled back. "Do you want to know what the investigator said?"

He obviously hadn't discovered the reason for her flight to the States, or Leiandros wouldn't still be blaming her for Dion's death. Or, would he? Her body trembled and she despised the outward sign of her susceptibility to his words and his touch. "Yes."

He moved his hand, but only to rest it on her hip. He cupped her nape with his other hand, effectively trapping her within his arms. "You don't date. Ever. Not once in the three years since a certain window watching, elderly neighbor moved into the house across the street from your own."

Savannah felt vulnerable by his knowledge of her social life. "Who I date, or if I date is no concern of yours."

She hadn't dated at first because she'd been married, but even after Dion had died, her fear of men had not. Where was that fear now? Why wasn't it protecting her from Leiandros's potent attraction?

The hand on her nape squeezed. "Everything about you is my concern. You are going to be my wife and the mother of my children."

"I'm not." If she said it often enough, perhaps he would believe her.

He didn't bother to argue. "She also said you are on the verge of nervous collapse."

"Ridiculous!"

He shook his head. "According to her, you sleep very little, spend too much time driving to and from Brenthaven and need more help with the girls than the full-time university student you hired."

Savannah felt exposed, as if her every secret had been laid as bare as a baby's bottom in the bath. "I can handle taking care of my daughters and a few sick room visits."

Okay, so maybe she'd looked a little worn around the edges by the time she and the girls had left for Greece, but saying she was on the verge of nervous collapse was just plain silly.

"Can you not see that marriage to me will benefit you? You have pushed yourself too hard for too long. I will take care of you. Here you have Cassia to help you care for the girls and they will have both a mother and a father, the way it should have been from the beginning."

Leiandros could not possibly know how strongly he had tapped into her deepest desire. She wanted a whole family, had always longed for one and had even married too young and foolishly in order to make her dream a reality. Only marriage to Dion had turned her dreams into nightmares. Was Leiandros offering anything different?

His hand felt warm and improbably comforting against her neck. "I can also finance your aunt's stay at Brenthaven."

"She needs me with her."

"The doctor said she does not remember who you are from one day to the next. She needs care, but not at *your* hand."

The words wounded because Savannah could not deny their truth. She bit back the sob welling in her throat, blinking to dispel the moisture gathering behind her eyes. She never cried and she wouldn't start now, in front of her enemy.

Last night's anomaly, she tried to forget.

"You need a resting period. You are tired and worn-out emotionally. Even I can see that and you've been in Greece no more than twenty-four hours."

She laughed bitterly. "Right. So, now you're motivated by consideration for me. Your vengeance has nothing to do with it and my frazzled emotions are all because of Aunt Beatrice. They have nothing to do with you and your attempt to *blackmail* me.''

The specter of being forced to play the part of a human incubator loomed larger in Savannah's mind than anything else at the moment. She could not face going through that kind of pain again. Every month she didn't conceive she would be accused of being a failure as a woman, of taking something to prevent conception, of emasculating her husband.

And she'd learned that conception had not ended the humiliating litany of woes against her. She had to have a *boy* baby. A Kiriakis heir. Leiandros would be as equally determined as Dion had been. He had lost a son and expected her to replace what he had lost.

He brushed his thumb over her ear and then, finally, pulled his hand away from her. ''I will have justice, Savannah. I am not looking for revenge. Justice does not negate the reality that you too will find certain benefits in our marriage.''

''Benefits...'' She let her voice trail off.

Is that how he saw it?

''Yineka mou.'' There was that endearment again. But she wasn't his woman. She wasn't his wife. ''Your body goes up in flames at my slightest touch. It will be no hardship for you making a child with me.''

Humiliated color stained her cheeks and she glared at him. ''What if I *can't?*'' she asked, hopelessness edging her voice.

''You have already given birth to two precious little girls. The evidence indicates that you will have no trouble conceiving. Petra was pregnant within two months of our decision to try for a baby. Why should it be any different for you?''

Savannah curled her arms protectively around her stomach, over her womb. ''But what if it is? What then?''

''Why are you worried about such a thing? Did you have surgery or something?'' Outrage at the thought laced his voice.

She sighed. ''I haven't had surgery. I've never taken the pill or had any device implanted to prevent conception,'' she listed off, remembering Dion's accusations when her menses had come month after month the first year they were married.

''Then we have nothing to concern us in this regard.''

If only he knew, but even now, Savannah felt shame when she thought of the placating role she'd played in her marriage and a part of her *had* felt less of a woman when she hadn't conceived easily that first time. ''I don't *want* to marry you.''

He shook his head and stood up. ''You're very stubborn.''

''Yes. And I won't marry you,'' she said, more forcefully.

''You will. You owe it to me. You owe it to Helena and Sandros. You owe it to Eva and Nyssa.''

She swung her feet around and stood. His last assertion had finally penetrated the wall she kept her anger safely locked behind. She owed her daughters safety and love. She did not owe them a place in a family which had rejected them once already and her as well.

''*I don't owe anyone anything.*'' She glared at him when he opened his mouth to speak and made a slicing gesture through the air with her hand. "Be quiet. You've had your say. Now, I'll have mine."

She could feel cleansing fury vibrating through her body. "It's not my fault that Dion drove while under the influence of alcohol. He made that decision. You made the decision to allow your young wife to maintain a friendship with an unstable man. If friendship was all it was."

She remembered too well Dion's favorite method of proving his masculinity when she failed to provide him with a son.

Leiandros seemed to swell with indignation and his six-foot-four-inch frame became even more intimidating than usual. *"Are you implying my cousin had an affair with my wife?"*

"Maybe. How would you know? By your own admission, you didn't love her. A woman finds emotion a seductive force." Who better than she to know how adept at projecting ardent affection Dion had been? She'd been taken in, hadn't she?

"You probably spent the minimum amount of time in Petra's company, Kiriakis International taking priority. No wonder she hooked up with Dion. He was closer to her age, good at the role of charming companion and was available where you were not."

Two slashes of red scored Leiandros's sculpted cheekbones and rage flashed out of his now almost black eyes. He took a step toward her and she flinched, but she didn't back away.

She was still too angry.

His hand swung up and she made a quick evasive maneuver, but he hadn't been about to strike her. His eyes narrowed and his finger pointed toward the door of the study. *"Get out."*

"Why? Is the truth so hard to hear? You want to blame me for your failure? Okay. Fine. But don't think I'll accept it. Don't think I'll marry you and become your broodmare because of it. You want another baby? Marry another Petra!"

"Leave. Now. Before I say something we both might regret." Each word shot out like a bullet from between his gritted teeth.

What could he say that would be more painful than what had already transpired? "Don't you mean do? Should I leave before you *do* something *I'll* regret?"

The need to taunt him beyond control rode her hard. What would he do in a towering rage? Would he use his fists when words did not work? "What will you *do*, Leiandros, if I refuse to leave? What will you *do* if I maintain my belief that your wife and my husband might have been more than friends?"

Her words seemed to infuriate him further. His expression turned deadly furious. "Are you implying now that I would strike you? Is it not enough that you seek to sully the memory of Petra and Dion with your vicious tongue without making me out to be some monster that would hit a woman?"

"Wouldn't you?" she goaded him further.

"No," he bit out. "I might kiss you to shut you up, but you like my kisses. I would never physically harm you."

His entire body radiated with incandescent fury. She had smeared his Greek honor, insulted his family and refused to take the words back. Still, he made no move to hurt her. He didn't even force the kiss on her he had threatened. He simply stood there, his anger like a living thing between them. His eyes demanded she acknowledge his words.

Something that had been locked tight inside Savannah for the past four years, opened and she said, "I believe you."

He could not know how difficult the words had been to say.

"Then believe me also when I tell you to go."

She went. Not because she feared him physically, but because she needed time to think.

Once Savannah left the study, she gave up any hope of time for contemplation. Eva and Nyssa wanted to explore the grounds, so Savannah found herself walking the pathways that had seemed so interesting to her the night before.

They were in an orchard of fig trees when Leiandros joined them. "I see you've found my favorite orchard." His smile did not include Savannah, but was focused on Eva and Nyssa.

"Theios!" Nyssa hurtled herself at him and was swung up in the air for a twirl before being lowered to the ground.

He ran his hand over Eva's hair. "Hello, quiet little girl. Do you and your sister like figs?"

Eva's eyes shone as she looked up at Leiandros. "Yes. May we try one? Is it safe?"

"Yes, *Theios,* please, can we try one?" Nyssa chimed in.

"It is safe. We do not use spray pesticides in our

groves or orchards.'' He picked two ripe figs for the
girls.

He turned to Savannah. ''Would you like one?''

''No, thank you.'' She met his gaze levelly. ''Did you
tell them to call you uncle?''

''Yes.'' He didn't elaborate, or ask her if that was all
right with her, but then he wouldn't.

Leiandros believed he knew what was best for every-
body.

Typically Eva finished her fig first. Nyssa had been
too busy chattering away, uncaring if anyone was listening. Eva moved close to Leiandros and touched him on
the arm. Savannah still had difficulty believing how
comfortable her shy daughter acted around the tall, powerful male.

''*Theios?*''

''Yes, little Eva?''

''I'm tired.''

''Then I think I should carry you.''

Eva smiled dazzlingly at this obviously correct response to her broad hint. ''That would be nice.''

Nyssa's face twisted with a frown. She silently
watched as Leiandros hoisted Eva's shorts clad figure to
his shoulder. ''I think Eva will not be tired in a little
while and then you can carry me, *Theios.*''

Savannah felt herself sharing Leiandros's obviously
amused reaction to Nyssa's logic. ''If you are tired,
sweetie, I can carry you now.''

Nyssa's brow furrowed. ''I don't think I'll get tired
till Eva's turn is over.'' Proving the truth of her words,
she turned to skip along the path between two rows of

fig trees. Leiandros followed, talking in low tones to Eva.

Alarmed at the ready acceptance her daughters were showing Leiandros, Savannah trailed behind. Would they be just as taken with Helena and Sandros? Was she wrong to want to take them back to Georgia, away from an extended family that could love them?

Eva and Nyssa didn't have any other close adult ties in their lives. Their school and Sunday school teachers changed every year. They had no grandparents, no aunts and uncles. Aunt Beatrice, who had been the lynchpin of Savannah's childhood had had Alzheimer's since before the girls were born. Savannah had been too busy and admittedly too leery to make any other close friendships.

She could see why Leiandros's case might have a favorable reception in court, but even more importantly she felt a searing guilt that she hadn't done more to make lasting relationships for her daughters to share in.

She realized that she'd lagged quite a ways behind the threesome when Leiandros stopped and turned towards her. "Are you coming *moro mou?*"

She frowned at the endearment and hurried to catch up.

"Why did you call Mama your baby?" Eva asked.

Leiandros turned his head up toward Eva's face. "How did you know this is what I called her?"

Eva looked at Leiandros with an expression that said he wasn't very bright, but she was too polite to say so and Savannah couldn't help being amused by it. "Because I know."

"You speak Greek?" He sounded incredulous.

Eva shrugged. "Of course I do."

"I do, too," Nyssa announced.

He spun to face Savannah. *"You taught them Greek?"*

He didn't need to make it sound like the eighth wonder of the world. She had reached the others and stopped a few safe feet from his masculine form. "Yes."

"*You* speak the language?"

"It would be difficult to teach them otherwise."

He frowned at her sarcasm.

She refused to be cowed. The Kiriakis family had always been quick to believe the worst of her. Why cater to his surprise she had learned Greek and subsequently taught it to her daughters? In the three years she'd lived in Athens, she had worked very hard at becoming proficient in her new home's native tongue. The tutor she had hired for the purpose had pronounced her fluent six months before she had left Greece.

She'd never shared her new skill with Dion. By the time she was fluent enough not to fear his ridicule at her attempts in his language, she had not cared enough about his opinion to try to win it by telling him.

"It's Greek at breakfast and bedtime and English in between," Eva offered.

Leiandros looked at Savannah, his expression for once very decipherable. He looked as shocked as she'd felt when he'd announced his intention to marry her. "You are teaching your daughters to speak my language?"

Typically arrogant. *His* language indeed. *"Yes."*

"Why?" he demanded.

She'd done it because she had known the skill would be one more protection for her daughters from wholesale rejection by their Greek relatives. She had also believed it was important for the girls not to be denied half of their heritage as Savannah's paternal heritage had been denied her.

"I didn't want to lose my own fluency through lack of use and bilingual abilities could only enhance the girls' futures," she said dismissively, unwilling to share her more personal reasons with him.

"*Theios?*"

Leiandros turned. "Yes, Nyssa?"

"You like children, huh?"

He looked over her head at Savannah. "Very much."

"You want your own. You said so," Eva quietly inserted.

His gaze did not waver from Savannah, his eyes telegraphing a message she did not want to hear. "Yes."

"Would it be just as good to have little girls that were already born?" Nyssa asked.

Shocked to the core of her being, Savannah's throat felt locked in silence.

"Yes. I think having two little girls would be very good." He sounded so sincere and the way he looked at Nyssa spoke volumes.

"Me and Nyssa like babies," Eva announced. "Do you want more babies, too?"

"Definitely." This time Leiandros did more than look at Savannah, he reached out and touched her. Just a small brush of his fingers against the flat of her stomach but the implication was unmistakable to her. He was claiming possession and Heaven help her, she felt possessed.

"If you married Mama, you'd be our daddy wouldn't you?" Nyssa asked, while Eva looked hopefully on.

"You could call me *bampas* instead of *theios*."

Delight radiated from both her daughters and Nyssa turned to Savannah. "Eva and me decided that since our other father is dead, it would be okay for you to get married and get us a real one. One who wants to play games with us and will carry us when we're tired. I'm not too heavy to sleep in *Theios's* lap."

Savannah closed her eyes against the expectant expression gracing the two little faces and the smug expression on the man's. She felt trapped by her love for her daughters, by Leiandros's strength of will and her own weakness toward him.

"I think it would be an excellent idea for your mama and I to get married. Would you like to see the chapel where I plan to marry your mama?"

CHAPTER SEVEN

THEY spent another hour viewing the grounds, Eva and Nyssa enthusiastically agreeing to Leiandros's suggestion they see the chapel. The same white stucco structure under a red tile roof as the villa, it was the size of a country church back home. The bell tower and mosaic cross above the door indicated the building's purpose with simple dignity.

The girls made heavy hints about the suitability of such a church for a fairytale wedding. After Leiandros's blatant statement of intent, Savannah had quickly disabused her daughters of the notion she had agreed to marry him and informed all three conspirators she was unwilling to discuss the subject any more that day. But by the time they left the chapel, Savannah felt hunted.

Approaching the villa, an unfamiliar sense of welcome assailed her. True to its name Villa Kalosorisma. Welcome house. She had never felt welcome in a Kiriakis home, not even Dion's apartment in Athens. The quintessential bachelor pad, he'd resisted every change she made to it in pursuit of a family *home.* Yet this big white Mediterranean villa inexplicably felt like *her place.* A refuge.

When they got inside, Leiandros lifted Nyssa from his shoulders, having made the switch with the girls at the chapel.

Cassia appeared, with a shy smile on her face. "Did you enjoy your time outdoors?"

"It's great here," Eva enthused, "with lots of places to play and run and everything's so pretty. I want to live here always. I like the pool and the Mediter...the Mederanian. I could have my own bedroom."

Eva's voluble reply seemed to stun Cassia, maybe because the little girl had said it all in Greek. Savannah felt similarly poleaxed. Her daughter might not be able to pronounce Mediterranean, but she certainly had no trouble expressing her desires when the need arose.

"Don't you like sharing a room with Nyssa?" Savannah asked.

"Yes, Mama, but if we each had our own rooms then we could make up more games to play, like having our own houses for playing neighbors."

Nyssa piped up with, "When Eva wants to read, I could tell stories to myself and she wouldn't get mad."

Eva turned to Leiandros. "Nyssa only reads a little bit, but I read really well." She wrinkled her nose. "Greek is harder, but Mama says I'm getting better."

Leiandros's gaze caught Savannah's. "I suppose you taught them to read early as well."

She shrugged in reply.

He said, "It sounds like they both know what they want."

Savannah had no recourse but to nod in agreement.

"Isn't it lucky for me they want the same thing I do?"

"It's what I want in the end that counts." Brave words, but not necessarily true. How could she ignore her daughters' clear desire to stay in Greece, particularly after being ignorant for so long about their wish for a father?

"But you'll be swayed by the needs they've expressed this afternoon and by doing what is best for them."

She couldn't deny his assessment, so she didn't bother. Shrugging again, she broke eye contact.

She shifted her gaze to Cassia. "Would you mind taking the girls up and giving them their baths before dinner?"

"Of course, *Kyria.*" Cassia led the girls up the stairs.

Savannah moved to go after them, craving a long, hot bath before overseeing her daughters' dinner and bedtime routine.

Leiandros stayed her with his hand on her shoulder. "I need to talk to you for a minute."

She refused to turn and face him, but the heat of his hand through her short cotton top resonated through her body. "If this is about the marriage vendetta, forget it. I've heard all I want on that subject."

"It is no vendetta." His hand gently squeezed her shoulder. If she didn't know better, she'd think he was trying to soothe the desperate edge to her voice. "I have arranged for us to dine with Helena and Sandros in Halkida this evening."

She felt her body turning of its own volition so she could see him once again. "Halkida?"

After a single caress of his thumb against her collarbone which sent her nerves tingling, he dropped his hand from her shoulder and nodded. He was always touching her and disturbing her equilibrium. "The island's capital. It is thirty minutes distant and close to their home."

She supposed she had known that, but right now she

really couldn't remember. With his attitude toward her and his certainty she would marry him, why bother trying to pretend he intended to keep his promise to let her determine whether or not Eva and Nyssa were to meet their grandparents?

She supposed this dinner was some sort of sop to his conscience. "What's the point?" she asked with resignation.

As her daughters' appointed guardian in Greece, he could force the issue and without doubt he would.

His mouth firmed in a straight line. "What do you mean?"

"You'll do what you want regardless of my feelings." She smoothed her hand down the bright yellow walking shorts that matched her top. "I don't see any point in a meeting them when you have already made the decision. I'm the wayward wife, the mother that took my babies to another country to live. I have no standing in your eyes and even less with Sandros and Helena."

His body went tense and she discovered he could exude just as much power in sexy tan polo and navy blue shorts as his handmade Italian suits. "I gave you my word."

Once again she'd insulted his Greek pride. She couldn't make herself care. "You also threatened me with all sorts of negative reprisals if I don't agree to your revenge scenario."

"Not revenge. Justice." He looked so darn serious, like he really believed his own justification.

He wasn't trying to hurt her, but right an imbalance. She'd have to marry him and have his baby to do it, but hey, that was the way the wheels of justice turned.

Sometimes they crushed, but they must roll to completion. He didn't even care if she loved him. Love played no part in his plans.

And if she did love him? If she had loved him for seven long years and he was the only man she would ever be able to trust her body with, what then? Talons of fear clawed her insides at the prospect that her inexplicable physical reaction to him and burgeoning trust in the face of his threats, indicated an altogether more devastating emotion than lust.

She didn't know if the panic she felt showed on her face, but she prayed it didn't. "You're saying if I feel it would be best for Eva and Nyssa *not* to meet their grandparents, you'll support my decision?"

"That is not going to happen." Such confidence.

"How can you be so sure? Because you believe no Kiriakis could do wrong? You weren't there the day Helena dismissed my baby, but I'll never forget it. I won't let my daughters face that kind of rejection again. Not ever."

He shook his head, negating her words with a gesture and she wanted to stomp her feet and scream. What did he know? She glared at him instead, surprising herself. Since her return to Greece, but particularly after their confrontation in the study, she'd felt her rigid emotional control slip away bit by bit. Especially when she was angry.

"When I showed them the pictures you had sent Dion, they both became emotional," he said. "They want very much to know their granddaughters."

"When did you show them the pictures?" she demanded, feeling oddly betrayed.

"Two weeks ago after our telephone call."

"You mean the call where you *blackmailed* me into bringing my daughters to Greece? The one where you promised me it would be *my choice?*" she asked, her voice dripping with sarcasm.

"It will be your choice," he said through gritted teeth.

"So you *will* support me if I refuse?" she pushed.

"Yes," he bit out.

The journey from Villa Kalosorisma to his cousins' home was accomplished in silence once Leiandros accepted that all of his overtures toward Savannah would be met with one-word answers and preoccupation. She acted like he was taking her to stand trial rather than dinner with family.

She perched stiffly on the opposite seat and looked out the tinted windows with such intense focus, he found himself following her gaze more than once to see what held her interest so completely. He saw only trees and stretches of coastline, nothing that electrifying.

Nothing worth ignoring him for, but then she would probably find any excuse to do that very thing.

She'd dressed in another of her simple, but elegant outfits, this time wearing an oversized sheer white shirt over her red sleeveless dress and racy red pumps with a tiny, high heel. She'd pulled her hair up into another of those loose, sexy styles that left a few soft brown strands flirting with her nape. His fingers stung with the need to touch her.

Even sitting with her knees so primly together, she could not hide her innate sensuality. The hem of her dress had ridden up to expose shapely thighs, but she did not fidget with the fabric. Just as earlier she had worn that enticingly short top that displayed glimpses of skin above the waistband of her shorts whenever she reached for one of the girls.

She blushed and could not bring herself to say the word "bra" in his presence and yet she showed no such embarrassment about her body. What a puzzle she was.

"We should be at Sandros's home in a few minutes."

She nodded, her attention still on the scene out the window. "I know. I recognize the road."

"Dion did not take you to visit the family very often."

"No."

"Is that why you are so nervous tonight?"

She turned to face him, her eyes revealed nothing. She'd erected that emotionless façade of hers again. "I'm not nervous so much as lacking in pleasant anticipation."

He bit back a retort. He had to accept that she did not see his family as he did any more than she saw her own culpability in the events of a year ago. "It will be fine. You must trust me, Savannah."

"Must I?" Her glorious green eyes fixed on him with the same intensity she had shown for her vigil at the window. "I'm not sure that would be a smart thing for me to do."

"I do not want to hurt you and I will not allow anyone to hurt Eva and Nyssa. I give you my solemn vow." He waited to see how she would respond to his words.

He didn't understand himself. Why should it matter to him if she trusted him? She'd already insulted his pride and his honor on several occasions. Would she continue with her stubborn unwillingness to recognize the role he was assuming in her life? That of protector and lover.

She licked her red tinted lips. "Thank you."

At last she had chosen to accept his words rather than challenge them. He wanted to kiss her luscious mouth to seal this new tentative bond of trust and had even started to move from his seat when the limo slid to a halt. His chauffeur got out to fetch Sandros and Helena.

Savannah paled and the red of her lips took on a garish glare against the now pallid complexion of her face.

"You will trust me," he told her, uncomfortable with this additional sign of vulnerability in a woman he had been convinced was completely lacking in that commodity.

She closed her eyes and took a deep breath, letting it out slowly before opening them again. "I think I do and that scares me more than this meeting with my former in-laws."

Why should she be afraid to trust him? He was head of his family, trusted by them all to act in their best interests. Why did she find it so difficult to do the same? Okay, so he'd used threats to back up his proposal of marriage. Any businessman would do the same. He had learned early to use every possible weapon or inducement at his disposal when going after something he wanted, whether in Kiriakis International or his personal life. So he'd done the same with Savannah.

He wanted marriage. He wanted his children planted in her womb. He wanted justice. So, he had found her weak spots and capitalized on them, but that did not negate the truth of the benefits she would find in marriage to him. And according to her friend back in the states, she needed looking after. He'd been looking after his family for years, he could look after Savannah and her daughters as well.

Sandros and Helena came toward the car, walking behind the chauffeur.

"Iona is with them," Savannah said with accusation.

Impatience with her constant mistrust of every member of the Kiriakis family but most particularly him edged his voice when he spoke. "I didn't invite her, but she is your sister-in-law and seven years your junior. She's hardly a threat."

Savannah's expression went blank and distant and she looked away from him toward the others. "It doesn't matter."

Damn it. Why did he feel like a heel, now? He hadn't said anything wrong and yet he felt as if he'd let her down. He went through a litany of curses in his head. He was getting too protective. Savannah would have to deal with her fears and accept that her family would no longer allow her to dismiss them from her life.

He nodded. "I'm glad you realize that."

She didn't bother to reply and the door opened. Savannah scooted to the far end of the seat. Helena stepped inside, greeted Leiandros with a hug and kisses before sitting at the far side of Savannah's seat.

Iona got in, her smile bright. "Good evening, cousin. Mama invited me to join you tonight. I hope you don't mind?"

He gave her a kiss of greeting. "Not at all."

She slid onto the seat next to him. "You're wonderful."

He laughed, so busy with Iona, it took him several seconds to realize Savannah had gone absolutely rigid as Sandros took the seat beside her and insisted on greeting her with the traditional kiss on each cheek. The expression on her face was a stiff imitation of a smile.

He could see her mentally preparing herself and then lean forward to return the old man's greeting with a hasty peck on one cheek and then pulling away completely. At that moment, Leiandros realized two things. One, Neither Helena, nor Iona had bothered to greet Savannah in any way and two, she did not want to be sitting next to Sandros.

He watched as she drew completely into herself and moved a little further away from Sandros, creating a separate space from the other occupants in the limo as effectively as if she had erected a physical barrier.

Why hadn't he considered this possibility? He knew how skittish around men she was. She'd practically fallen over in her haste to get away from his touch at the airport and when she'd woken in his arms later in the car, she'd vaulted away, literally bouncing against the far wall.

He took for granted her swift transition to accepting his touch, but now realized it did not mean she was any more comfortable forced into close proximity to another male. She showed every sign of being a woman who had been abused. Had one of her lovers hurt her?

The thought infuriated him. He wanted to demand an explanation immediately, but could not. Nor could he do anything about her skittishness with Sandros without causing grave offense to innocent people. He fixed his gaze on her, willing her to look at him. He wanted her to remember he was with her and he would protect her.

A man had an obligation to do that for his woman and it had nothing to do with maudlin emotions or even affection, he reminded himself.

During his ruminations, Helena and Iona had started a discussion of the latest fashions in Greek that was clearly meant to exclude Savannah. Iona made a comment about the coarseness of the way some American women dressed which Helena agreed with. They did not realize Savannah understood, but that did not excuse their behavior.

Sandros sat in silence, his expression faintly troubled.

Leiandros said, "Since the purpose of this evening is for Savannah to become reacquainted with the family, I think it would be best if you included her in your conversations, Helena."

"Yes, of course." Her voice lacked enthusiasm.

Iona snorted.

Sandros glared at his daughter and patted his wife's hand. "Remember, English."

Leiandros donned the expression he wore to deal with offending employees and met first Helena's eyes and then Iona's. "That won't be necessary. Perhaps you are ignorant of the fact, as I was, but Savannah worked very hard at becoming fluent in Greek and has even taught her daughters to speak our language. The oldest is learning to read in it as well."

"Did she tell you that?" Iona asked with sneering derision. "Really, Leiandros, I wouldn't expect you of all people to be so gullible. The oldest can be no more than five. A child that age simply isn't capable of such a thing."

He saw Savannah flinch out of the corner of his eye and realized Iona would ruin any chances Helena and Sandros had for visitation with her youthful emotionalism. "You are wrong, Io. I can assure you both girls are fluent in our language because I've spoken with them at length in Greek and Eva does indeed read it as she proved to me when I tucked her in for the night."

Iona turned to regard Savannah for the first time. "How clever of you. Isn't it a tragedy you didn't bother to share your abilities with your *husband?*"

Feeling his frustration mount, he said, "Io, either decide to be a pleasant dinner companion, or accept that I will send you home in a taxi when we reach the restaurant."

Her eyes filled with tears. "It's not fair! You're treating us like criminals when she's the one who's done everything wrong. It's sheer conceit for her to demand a meeting to determine whether my parents and I are worthy of having a part in Dion's daughters' lives."

"Their names are Eva and Nyssa. They are human beings with thoughts, feelings and needs. They are not possessions to be fought over like some disputed piece of jewelry. Eva is the oldest. Your mother met her once. Nyssa is a year younger and did not have the benefit of even one meeting." Savannah's voice dripped with ice.

Helena's expression grew drawn and strained as Savannah's words penetrated, but Sandros looked as if he had the guilt of original sin on his shoulders. Iona opened her mouth to say something but Leiandros forestalled her.

"Let us get something clear. Savannah is not responsible for this meeting. I am. I am the one who extended the invitation to your parents. I am the one who allowed you to accompany us and I am beginning to wonder if that was a mistake. You're responding like an adolescent."

Iona gasped and instead of glaring at him, gave Savannah a look meant to wound. "I know Leiandros only agreed to this meeting because *you* forced him to."

Leiandros squeezed Iona's arm to warn her to silence. "As Dion's chosen legal guardian for his daughters and head of this family, it is my responsibility to make certain Eva and Nyssa's best interests are served."

Sandros nodded. "Exactly right."

Leiandros waited a second in silence to give his upcoming words impact. "I do not think encouraging a relationship with family members who dislike their mother and treat her with open scorn, would be beneficial in any way to Eva or Nyssa."

"Leiandros, you can't mean you would stand behind her scheming to keep us from our blood family," Helena said.

Iona nodded her agreement so vehemently, she looked like her head was attached to her body with a bobbing spring.

Sandros shifted in his seat, inadvertently moving closer to Savannah. "If Leiandros does not do as he's said, I will. No granddaughter of mine is going to be subjected to the kind of scene that's taken place in this car. Neither my wife nor my daughter exercised simple courtesy in greeting the mother of those little girls and the conversation so far has been distasteful.'' He subsided in silence.

''When have any of you ever known me to back down on my word?'' Leiandros asked for Savannah's benefit.

''Never,'' Iona admitted grudgingly.

''Of course you keep your word,'' Helena replied, her voice expressing outrage at the question.

''Then accept that welcoming your granddaughters into your life will come after you have made your peace with Savannah.''

Iona moved away from him, crossing her arms in a childish expression of defiance. Imagine she was of an age to marry. He pitied her future husband.

His eyes moved to lock Helena in his gaze.

''I will make every effort,'' she said.

Sandros once again patted her hand. ''*Yineka mou*, you are a wife worthy of respect.''

Savannah hadn't made a peep since Sandros had moved so close to her, but she was practically crawling onto the armrest.

''Iona, trade places with Savannah. You've made it clear you would be more comfortable sitting beside your father.'' He would normally ignore her little gestures of annoyance, but he could not stand that stiff lip and blank-eyed stare on Savannah's face for one second longer.

Io got up without deigning to answer. Savannah remained seated, clearly in a different world entirely.

''Savannah. *Pethi mou*. Come here.''

Her eyes opened wide as if waking from a dream and she stared at him, their green depths dark with the emotions swirling through her. ''Come to you?''

Iona made an impatient movement. "Don't act stupid. A woman capable of teaching her children to speak Greek and read before they are even six years old can understand a simple command."

Leiandros did not take issue with Iona because she had complimented Savannah, backhanded though it might be. He put his hand out toward Savannah and she vaulted off the seat, ducking under Io to take the spot next to him, her thigh touching his own.

He took her hand in his and brushed against her palm with his thumb. She shivered and pressed herself closer.

"Thank you," she whispered under her breath.

He squeezed her hand. He liked the way it felt when she aligned herself with him, too much. Her gratitude could become addictive.

CHAPTER EIGHT

AFTER the events in the car, it took several minutes for Savannah to become more than peripherally aware of her elegant surroundings. Sandros had suggested dining in a restaurant connected to a five-star hotel and it showed. Fine linen, crystal and delicate china graced the table at which they sat. She had no doubt the food would be up to the same standards of excellence. Not that she cared.

After the scene in the car and the humiliatingly tortuous experience of being forced to sit so closely to Sandros, she had no appetite and even less desire for the ordeal to come.

Leiandros laid a casual arm across the back of her chair, his fingers brushing her shoulder through the light silk of her overblouse. Did he have any idea the effect his touch had on her? Volts of electricity shot down her arm as his touch sparked something very different than the comfort he so clearly intended.

"Relax, *pethi mou*. All will be well."

She took a deep breath and tried to obey him, but she was fighting both trepidation over the meeting to come and her body's susceptibility to him. Under the cover of Sandros giving his order to the waiter, she asked, "How can you think so? They hate me. What hope is there for Nyssa and Eva?"

Almost black eyes burned into hers. "Your daughters

are separate people. Their grandparents love them already just from their pictures. Imagine how besotted they will become when they meet your sweet-natured daughters in person.''

Which meant what exactly? That all his fine words in the car meant nothing and it did not matter if Dion's family hated her guts as long as they could love Eva and Nyssa?

The waiter had turned to Leiandros, who requested a bottle of Greek wine and then proceeded to order for Savannah and himself with typical arrogance.

She had no opportunity to pursue her discussion with him before the waiter returned with their wine. Leiandros deferred tasting to Sandros and Savannah remembered Dion saying his father was something of an expert on wines, particularly those native to Greece. Sandros pronounced the wine acceptable and gave the waiter permission to pour.

As the waiter approached her, Leiandros asked, ''Would you prefer a spritzer?''

She needed to keep her wits about her tonight. ''Yes.''

''That's enough,'' he told the waiter when her glass was a third full. ''Please bring us a club soda.''

''Are our Greek wines too strong for your palate?'' Iona's voice was heavy with derision and Savannah's throat tightened.

Leiandros sighed. ''I think it is time for me to call you a taxi, Iona. You refuse to be civil and clearly do not have the maturity to realize that your sniping is only making a difficult situation worse.''

Did he think sending Iona away would solve the basic problem?

Shockingly, Iona's sarcastic mask crumbled and tears shimmered in her dark eyes. "I'm sorry."

Leiandros's expression did not soften. "I told you what would happen in the car if you continued to bait Savannah."

Iona turned her tear wet face toward her father. "Papa, please don't let Leiandros send me away. I am family, too."

If anything, Sandros's expression was even more forbidding. "Leiandros is well within his rights to send you home."

A small sob escaped Iona, now looking much younger and much more vulnerable than she had earlier. "Mama?" she pleaded.

When Helena remained silent, Savannah laid her hand on Leiandros's arm and spoke. "I prefer that Iona stay."

Leiandros's gaze turned to her, blasting her with censure. "You do not want this to work," he accused her in a tone so low only she could distinguish the words. "You are looking for a reason to withhold your daughters from their rightful family just as you withheld them for the past four years."

She supposed to his way of thinking, taking her daughters halfway around the world had effectively cut them off from their family, but pain at his words still coursed through her. He'd turned on her so easily. Was she right in believing he didn't care how repulsed Dion's family was by her?

Her feelings did not matter. Her pain could be dismissed. After all, she was the cuckoo. Everyone else at this table belonged. Even the volatile Iona. Savannah was the interloper and always would be. She'd never belonged, really belonged to anyone but Aunt Beatrice and then Eva and Nyssa.

Even that was being undermined here. Leiandros wanted Eva and Nyssa to belong to the Kiriakises as much as, or maybe more than, they belonged to Savannah and in a way she never could. They would never accept her. Would giving her daughters an extended family sentence her to a lifetime of rejection?

"Can you honestly say that any relationship between my daughters and their grandparents will not include Iona?" she whispered back, refusing to give into the despair boiling up inside of her.

Her only hope was to hold Leiandros to his word, even as he tried to manipulate her into letting him break it.

Surprisingly, his expression turned thoughtful.

She took her hand off his arm, her fingers still tingling from the contact. "You are wrong, you know. I *am* aware they are the only extended family my daughters can lay claim to. If I can bring Dion's family into Eva and Nyssa's lives without hurting them, I will be happy to do so." Even if it meant the sacrifice of her own feelings.

The waiter arrived with her club soda.

She broke eye contact with Leiandros to thank the waiter and then poured the soda water into her wine. "You're right, Iona," she forced herself to say civilly, "Greek wine has its own unique essence and requires adjusting of the palate to truly appreciate its flavor."

Iona, who looked stunned by Savannah's defense of her right to stay, gave a weak smile.

A low, but persistent beeping prevented further discussion as Leiandros pulled out his cell phone and answered with the traditional Greek words for greeting. He swiftly changed to a language that sounded like Italian.

Seconds later, he stood and gave them an encompassing glance of apology. "I'm sorry. I have to take this call. I'll make it as quick as possible." He leaned close to Savannah's ear. "Be good, *pethi mou.*"

She wasn't the one he had to worry about.

Sandros waved him away, while Savannah tried to hide the nervousness his abandonment was causing her. Even angry, she preferred Leiandros over dealing with Dion's family.

Silence reigned as she and the remaining guests at the table considered one another warily.

Helena put down her *dolmades* without taking a bite and looked across at Savannah with wounded eyes. "Why? Why did you tell my son the babies were not his? He missed so much. We all missed so much."

Resentment toward Dion welled up inside Savannah, but what good did anger toward a dead man do?

She met Helena's eyes, her own steady. "I never said any such thing. If you will recall, Helena, it was you who took one look at my beautiful Eva and declared her no Kiriakis." She turned to sear Iona with her gaze. "Is it any wonder I felt it necessary to meet with you all before I expose my daughters to possible rejection or revilement?"

"We would never do such a thing," Helena exclaimed.

"But Dion said you were unfaithful!" Iona said at the same time.

Savannah chose to answer Iona, ignoring Helena's blatantly untrue assertion. "I wasn't unfaithful. Ever."

Iona said, "But—"

Savannah cut her off, unwilling to travel this territory again. She'd already gotten bruised doing so with Leiandros. "I am not responsible for your brother's jealous delusions."

Feeling so brittle she thought she might shatter, Savannah bit back further, more precise words of self-defense. While an insidious voice in her mind demanded she acknowledge that in a way, Dion *had* been right. Oh, she had not encouraged other men. She hadn't been a flirt, but she had betrayed Dion. At least in her heart, because she had wanted his cousin.

She had wanted Leiandros Kiriakis with an obsession that had taken her entire strength of will to stifle, never allowing her fantasies to stray, ignoring the frisson of feeling his slightest touch could elicit, pretending her body did not hum with renewed life when he walked into a room she occupied.

She was shocked from her self-castigating musings when Sandros nodded in apparent agreement to her statement. "He was jealous because of his own feelings of failure, not because you gave him reason to be."

Sandros knew about Dion's low sperm count? Savannah could not believe it. Dion had been so adamant no one find out, ever, that he had made her life a misery in the pursuit of a son to prove his virility. After all that, had he told his father?

"Sandros! What are you saying?" Helena demanded, her cheeks flushed with distress.

Sandros gave a very heavy, very Greek sigh, looking

weary and sad. "Our son came to see me the morning of the accident."

"You never told me this," Helena said, her evident shock no greater than Savannah's.

"I could not." He squeezed Helena's hand. "He told me he had called Savannah the night before and asked her to bring their daughters to Greece. She refused."

Iona and Helena's hostility became a palpable entity.

Savannah did not want to defend herself to Dion's family, but if she refused to make an effort their current impasse could not be broken. "I invited Dion to come to Atlanta and visit the girls there." She had not trusted Dion not to take advantage of Greek family law to force her into keeping the girls in Greece.

Pity she hadn't been as savvy when dealing with Leiandros, but then deep down, she *had* wanted to see him again. She'd had no such desire regarding Dion.

"He told me this." Sandros grimly went on, "He said he considered the offer generous. I must admit I did not agree with him at first, but after he admitted to me that he had lied about Savannah's behavior and told me the separation was entirely his fault and why, I saw the truth in his belief that Savannah had behaved generously toward him."

"But she took the babies to America, so far away from family." Helena's voice cracked with emotion on the last word.

Sandros took both her hands in his own. "He admitted to me he refused to accept his role as a father because of his own self-doubt. He was obsessed with having a son."

He lifted his head and met Savannah's stricken gaze.

His eyes pleaded with her not to say anything more explicit. She was convinced he knew the whole truth about Dion's violent nature and it shamed him. He wanted to protect Helena and Iona from that shame.

She nodded her head slightly in acknowledgment and saw relief flicker in Sandros's eyes.

"Dion was young when we married, unprepared for his family's disapproval of his wife," she said, voicing the conclusion she'd drawn when trying to understand her former husband's behavior. "It is only natural that he sought to lay blame at my door. He didn't want to be alienated from those he loved so much."

She no longer believed Dion had ever loved her. She was convinced he had married her in an act of rebellion against having his entire future mapped out for him, including the choice of his bride.

Sandros grimaced. "You are too understanding, but my son guaranteed we would despise you from the beginning."

"What do you mean?" Savannah inquired, certain she was about to be regaled with another of Dion's lies.

"He told us you had gotten yourself pregnant and trapped him in marriage," Helena said, her voice questioning.

Savannah couldn't help laughing. "That would have been really something. The second immaculate conception on record." Though nothing Dion could have done could have surprised her, knowing he had undermined her relationship with his family in this way from the very beginning still hurt.

No wonder Leiandros had such a low opinion of her.

Helena and Iona gasped when the import of her words penetrated. Sandros looked pained.

"That's not possible," Iona practically shouted. "Dion told us he'd been a real chump, not requiring proof when you said you were pregnant. He said you'd lied to trap him, but if you were still chaste, he would not have believed you."

She took a sip of her spritzer, ignoring the humus and flat bread in front of her. "I guess he was trying to protect himself from his original lie being found out. I imagine he felt pretty desperate when I didn't conceive right away."

Only she knew how desperate.

She bit her tongue to prevent herself from saying more. Nothing would be served by accusing Dion of having been a selfish, manipulative, spoiled little boy during their marriage.

"Yes," Sandros said heavily. "The morning he came to see me, I told him the measure of a man is how he treats his family, not his ability to produce sons. I believe he was drinking later that day because of my words. It was the first time I was ever ashamed of him." Tears glistened in Sandros's eyes. "My son lied about his wife and he admitted those lies to me. We have all treated Savannah and her daughters shamefully because of the things Dion told us. The lies he told us."

Savannah couldn't help feeling compassion for his obvious feelings of guilt over his son's death. "You are not to blame."

"Papa, what is this you are saying?" Iona's voice shook.

"You said *nothing* of this a year ago." Helena reiterated.

His proud gray head bowed. "There are some things a man is not pleased to admit."

Savannah's heart ached for him as his head came up again and she saw the tears trickle down his cheeks, tears he wiped away with his thumb and forefinger.

Her half-formed idea that she would ask him to tell Leiandros the truth died a swift death. She could not ask Sandros to shred his pride in admitting Dion's weaknesses or his own to Leiandros. The Kiriakises had paid too high a price for Dion's sins already. None of which were their fault.

Helena's rejection of Eva had hurt Savannah, desperately so. Yet, how could Savannah blame the older woman for a reaction predestined by her beloved son's lies? The answer was that she couldn't. Nor could she withhold Eva and Nyssa from their Greek family when that family showed every evidence of wanting to love and cherish the little girls.

Surely now that Sandros had told Helena and Iona that Dion had lied about Savannah, their overt hostility toward her would end. Perhaps they would never be the best of friends, but they could maintain a relationship for the sake of two little girls who deserved more out of life than the loneliness Savannah had known.

One day, she would tell Leiandros the truth herself. All of it. He knew she hadn't dated in at least three years because her nosy neighbor had told his investigator as much. With that knowledge, he *couldn't* still see her as the unfaithful slut Dion had painted her.

Taking another fortifying sip of wine, she contemplated what to say next. "That is all in the past. We have to focus on the present. Eva and Nyssa deserve it. We all deserve it."

Sandros, more in control, nodded. "We all loved Dion, but he was no saint. We lost years of Eva and Nyssa's life because of mistaken beliefs. Let the anger and accusations end now." He spread his hands in a typically Greek expansive gesture.

It was Helena's turn to blink back moisture. She wasn't completely successful. "I want to hold my granddaughters."

Iona's eyes were troubled and she played with her fork. "I still don't understand why Dion would have lied to us."

Savannah didn't have an answer, so she said nothing. She'd gone as far as she could go in the reconciliation. The rest was up to Dion's family.

Leiandros chose that moment to return to the table, taking his chair beside Savannah. "My apologies I was gone so long."

"We hardly noticed," Savannah couldn't resist saying, though it was far from the truth. She noticed every moment she spent away from him and part of her wished he'd been there to witness Sandros's admissions about Dion. On the other hand, she had to wonder if Sandros would have hesitated to say anything in front of Leiandros. Male pride could be a very tricky thing.

Leiandros's dark brows rose in mockery. "Really?" Then he surveyed the table. "You haven't eaten anything."

"We have been talking," Sandros replied.

Leiandros's head twisted toward Savannah and he

searched her face, looking for she knew not what. Evidence of her capitulation, maybe? "We have all agreed it is time my daughters met their grandparents and aunt."

Rather than the satisfaction she expected to see, his expression became more probing. He reached out and laid his forefinger along her jaw. Even angry with him, she could not repress the immediate response of her body to his most innocent caress. "Are you okay with this?"

She jerked her face away. "Don't bother trying to pretend it matters to you," she said sharply, but in a very low voice she hoped the others could not hear. She still hadn't forgiven him for his earlier words.

His body tensed and he did not bother to whisper when he answered. "It does. I thought I convinced you of that before we left the house and did my actions not show you my sincerity earlier this evening?"

"Your actions showed me that you were intent on effecting a reconciliation even at the cost of protecting a woman you despise, but so you know, I *am* okay with this."

He looked like he wanted to say more, but Helena spoke up. "Savannah, do you think you could bring the children to our home in the next couple of days. I'm impatient to get to know them."

She stiffened at the prospect of visiting Helena's home with the girls, but she couldn't allow her own feelings stop her daughters from knowing important people in their lives who wanted to love them. "I'm sure they'd be happy to meet you tomorrow. Perhaps Leiandros would allow us to use his car to make the trip."

He shook his head and focused his attention on Helena and Sandros. "You are welcome at Villa Kalosorisma any time, but until Eva and Nyssa have come to know you and are sufficiently comfortable in your company, we shall hold off a visit for them to your lovely home."

While Helena nodded her agreement, her expression pained, Savannah tried to gather her thoughts scattered by Leiandros's unexpected announcement. He was putting Eva and Nyssa's needs above the feelings of his other family. She didn't fool herself into believing he'd done it for her sake.

He'd been as taken with her daughters as they had been with him.

CHAPTER NINE

LEIANDROS waited until Sandros and the other women had exited the limo before turning to Savannah. He touched her hand with his forefinger, running the tip along her soft skin. "The meeting was difficult for you."

She snatched her hand away. "Yes."

He stifled a sigh. She was back to bristling. She'd been angry with him since his return to the table from his phone call, accusing him of not caring whether or not she was okay with the results of the discussion which had occurred while he was gone. He had kept his word to her, but she didn't seem to see it that way. Angry he was forcing her hand about marriage, she gave him no credit at all.

"Yet you were kind to them, generous with the prospect of them getting to know the girls." It had surprised him after the way she had reacted to Io's sarcasm and his decision to send her home in a taxi.

She shrugged, her transparent shirt moving over the deep red of her dress. "My concerns were allayed in that regard."

"Your fear they would reject your daughters as they had once rejected you or your belief they would go on hating you?"

She bit her lower lip, breaking his concentration. He wanted to soothe that small wound with his tongue.

When she said, "Both," he could no longer remember

what the question had been. He had to concentrate to recall his words.

"They seemed to have dropped all hostility toward you, even Iona." The about face wholesale acceptance of Dion's family toward Savannah puzzled him.

He had expected a softening sooner or later. He knew how tenderhearted Helena and Iona really were. Their anger toward Savannah had been fed by their loyalty to Dion. With the advent of Eva and Nyssa into the family, new loyalties would be forged and regardless of Savannah's past treatment of Dion, she was now the mother of two little girls very much desired by their grandparents and aunt.

Yet, he had not expected the thaw to happen quite so quickly and had spent most of his phone call worried about the way his family was treating Savannah.

Something came and went in her expression. "You were right. They are very emotional at the prospect of getting to know Eva and Nyssa."

She shifted restlessly on the seat beside him and when she tried to move away, he anchored her against his hip with an arm around her waist. His hand curled over her lower rib cage and the feel of the sheer silk top against his fingers teased him. A slight upward move and his thumb would be caressing the delicate underswell of her breast.

He felt sweat break out on his brow. *He wanted to make that movement.* She knew it too. She had gone still and started breathing in short pants. He leaned down to nuzzle her ear, allowing his tongue to flick out and taste the tender flesh of her lobe as he bit it gently. "You taste good, *yineka mou.* Just as a woman should."

He wanted to taste more than this small morsel of her flesh. His body craved the opportunity to savor her lips and the silken warmth of her mouth, the golden softness of her skin, and her nipples. Most certainly, yes, her nipples. From there his tongue would travel a path to the womanly softness of her belly, to her inner thighs and the backs of her knees. He would take off her shoes and explore her dainty arches with his lips before returning to the secrets hidden between her thighs.

"We've been through this before. I'm not your woman. I'm not your wife."

It took him a second to retrieve his mind from the erotic journey it had been on and decipher what she had said. When he did, it was all he could do not to growl in frustration.

He kissed along the graceful line of her jaw while moving his hand up and under the transparent shirt, to cup her breast through the lightweight fabric of her dress. "You're wrong."

Her nipple puckered immediately and she sucked in air like a runner after a ten-kilometer dash. "Stop," she breathed.

He smiled in triumph and gently pinched the turgid nub.

She arched her back. "Leiandros! Please."

He tilted her face toward him so he could kiss her soft, sweet mouth. In the dark interior of the limo, her beautiful green eyes looked black and very, very wide.

He brushed her cheek. "Relax."

His lips prevented more half-hearted protests, not that she would have made any. The second his mouth touched hers, she melted against him in surrender. Her

lips softened and parted to allow her delightful little
tongue to dart out and trace his lips before teasing his
mouth open. He let her explore, meeting her tongue with
his own. She moaned and he pulled her closer, while
squeezing her breast in his hand. He wanted to touch her
without the fabric of her dress in the way.

He shoved her shirt off over her shoulders. The gar-
ment got stuck at her wrists and he left it there while
atavistic excitement at her hampered movement coursed
through him.

"I want you, Savannah." His voice sounded guttural
and out of control even to his own ears.

His hands were busy with the zipper on the back of
her dress when she responded.

"Do you really want *me*, or just an incubator for your
baby?" she demanded in a passion raw voice.

Even in his desire clouded mind, he could tell the
answer was important to her, and therefore to him. He
would not let her go. "I want *you*."

"Are you sure?"

The insecurity he heard in her voice told him she
would not be satisfied with words. He would have to
show her. He kissed her while lowering the zip on her
dress. When it was open, he pulled back and she groaned
her distress at the lack of contact.

A zing of primitive satisfaction shot straight to his sex
and he yanked the dress down to her elbows, increasing
the restriction of movement in her arms and hands. His
carnal hunger grew as he realized she was so lost to her
passion, she didn't even notice.

"*Pethi mou.* You are stunning," he whispered, as he
looked his fill at her exquisite body.

Tight, pointed tips, rosy with sensual excitement crested her luscious, golden mounds.

She said nothing, her own gaze fixed on his face. Her nostrils flared in primal recognition of him and her mouth parted, her lips swollen and begging for his kisses.

He obliged her, devouring her mouth with unrestrained hunger. She didn't resist, but kissed him back with the same frantic energy, the same fundamental sexual craving. His hands traveled to the bare flesh of her breast and he cupped them, letting his thumbs brush back and forth, back and forth, over her taut nipples. He could explode touching her like this.

She pressed herself into his hands.

He moved his lips down her jaw toward the irresistible call of her naked flesh. "Yes. *Moro mou.* That's right. Just like that," he said as she moved side to side to increase the friction of his touch on her tender flesh.

She was his fantasy woman, the lover of his dreams. So responsive. So sensual. He wanted her. *He needed her.*

The constriction on her hands and arms seemed to register for the first time as she tried to lift them. She moved in agitation, her head tossing against the back of the seat.

She whimpered and primitive pleasure washed over him in crashing waves. "What is it?"

"I want to touch you," she moaned.

His lips closed over a hardened nub and he sucked it into his mouth in one strong, swift action. He played with her using his teeth and tongue and her whimpers grew, this time filled with obvious pleasure as well as frustration.

"Oh, Leiandros! Please. I need you," she cried.

He needed her too. So much that he didn't know if he could take the time to remove their clothes before taking her. He moved to her other breast and administered the same treatment, exulting in her wildly thrashing body and incoherent demands.

With impatient movements, he shoved her skirt to her waist and grabbed the side of her silk panties just as the car slid to a halt. She didn't seem to notice, her face contorted with feminine desire, her eyes closed, her entire body abandoned to the pleasure she found in his arms.

He wanted to curse in each of the five languages he spoke, but didn't have time. With more speed than finesse, he dragged her dress back into place and reached around her throbbing body to close the zip.

Her eyes opened. "Leiandros?"

"We have arrived at Villa Kalosorisma," he said in a voice made harsh by unsatisfied passion.

Her languid eyes looked blankly back at him for a full five seconds before they grew wide and she scrambled to a sitting position.

She struggled against her blouse, unable to pull it back up with the sleeves inside out over her hands. "Fix it. Hurry!"

He obeyed and had it back in place just as the chauffeur opened the door.

Leiandros got out, pulling Savannah from the limo with him. "We aren't finished."

Her eyes registered his statement of intent with a mixture of alarm and still smoldering desire. *"Good night."*

He gripped her shoulders. "Like hell it is good night."

Her eyes dilated. "I didn't mean—"

"Tonight, you become mine. You will never again say I have not the right to call you *yineka mou.*" No way was she dismissing him like some casual date after a party, not following the unrestrained response she'd given him in the limo.

Her lovely lips moved, but no sound came out. He didn't need her answer; he could read it in the way her body swayed toward his. He bent to kiss her as the front door swung wide.

"Leiandros! You have returned. And Savannah! My terrible son did not bother to tell me you were coming, or I would have been here to welcome you home." His mother stood, silhouetted in the light pouring from the open doorway, his worst nightmare when his body was aching to possess Savannah.

There would be no possession tonight, nor any other night until the wedding. Not if his mother had her say about it, and when had Baptista Kiriakis ever hesitated to have her say?

Savannah struggled to listen as Baptista rattled on in rapid Greek. Her welcome had been effusive with a warm hug and kiss of greeting on each of Savannah's cheeks.

"I'm so pleased you've come to stay." She patted Savannah's shoulder. "Having you and the little girls here will be so good for Leiandros. He works too much, that one.''

Baptista gave her son a censorious look.

His lips tilted cynically in reply.

"I'm very happy to be here," Savannah replied, unable to snub such open friendliness.

Baptista led them into the fireside reception room. "Come, let us have a nightcap before we retire. I have so much I wish to say to Savannah. My words for my son will wait for a more opportune time," she said ominously.

Savannah could almost pity him, but it was his fault she had to face Baptista, wondering how unkempt her own appearance was after their loss of control in the limo. More than merely a loss of control, it had been a life-altering experience. Still she did not want Baptista to know what they had been doing.

After insisting Leiandros pour them all a glass of champagne, *to celebrate Savannah's return to Greece,* Baptista pulled Savannah onto one of the sofas beside her.

"I met your daughters. I told them they must consider me their honorary grandmother." She gave Leiandros another judicious look. "That one may never get around to remarrying and providing me with grandchildren."

Savannah choked on her champagne, coughing and turning bright red as the oxygen rushed back to her head. What would Baptista think if she discovered her son wanted exactly that and was willing to resort to blackmail to get it?

He was there in a moment, seated on her other side, angled to face both her and his mother, his legs brushing against her own in a very distracting way. "Are you all right, *pethi mou?*"

She nodded, feeling distinctly vulnerable. She tried a tentative smile on him and his mother. "I'm not used to champagne," she said by way of a very lame excuse.

She hoped to shout she could come up with something better than that, otherwise Baptista was going to go to bed a very suspicious woman. Savannah stifled a groan at the thought.

Baptista's thin, lovely face warmed with a smile. Her lithe figure couldn't have been more different from Helena's voluptuous one and the already graying hair complimented Baptista's olive toned skin, while attesting to her age. With her luxuriant black locks, Helena looked young enough to be Iona's older sister.

But then the two older women were not related by blood. They had married Kiriakis cousins, though Leiandros treated Sandros and Helena more like a favored uncle and aunt.

"Eva and Nyssa are darlings. The little treasures greeted me in Greek. How clever you are to have mastered our language and then taught it to your children."

"Thank you," Savannah replied.

The other woman smiled apologetically at her son. "I think you ought to run along to bed, Leiandros. Savannah and I have so much to catch up on."

Savannah couldn't imagine what. She'd seen very little of Baptista Kiriakis her first time in Greece, though the older woman had always been kind to her. She turned to Leiandros, her expression as pleading as she could make it. She didn't want to be left alone with his mother.

He gave her a wry smile and shrugged. He was going to leave her. The polecat.

He leaned forward to kiss her forehead and even that innocuous salute caused her heart rate to increase. "Sleep well, Savannah. Pleasant dreams." He imbued the age old bedtime farewell with significance and personal meaning that had her insides melting even as his mother smiled benignly on them both.

He kissed his mother's cheek and bid her good night before leaving the room without another murmur.

"So…" Baptista's eyes measured Savannah and then she smiled with something that looked like satisfaction.

"Are you sleeping with my son, or is it still in the flirting stage?" she asked as Savannah tried hard not to fall off the couch in shock.

The next morning, Savannah was still reeling from Baptista's frank inquiries and equally frank assurances that the older woman wholly approved of the evident affection between her son and Savannah.

Turning onto her back on the sun lounger, Savannah lifted the upper portion of the chair to support her in a semireclining position. She surreptitiously watched Leiandros and the girls play together in the pool. Savannah had been swimming with her daughters when he came onto the terrace dressed in nothing more than a very sexy set of swimming trunks. He dove into the pool and she climbed out, leaving him to the mercy of two little girls with enough energy to light a small city.

She simply could not face the intimacy of joining in the water play after the way she'd come apart in his arms the night before.

Eva laughed at something Nyssa did and Leiandros went after both of them with a mock growl of outrage.

If she decided to marry him, he and the girls' strong rapport would make them a family in the true sense of the word, but where did she fit in?

Was she just a sacrifice on the altar of his perception of justice or did he truly want her for herself as he had passionately declared last night in the limo?

She silently ticked off the cons of marrying him on her fingers. He was ruthlessly blackmailing her into marriage. He didn't love her. He held her responsible for his cousin's death and that of his pregnant wife. A chill brought goose bumps to the surface of her skin. *He wanted her to replace his lost son.*

How would he react if Savannah only ever had daughters and more daughters? Would he resent it and blame her the way Dion had done? The prospect made her feel ill.

She watched as Leiandros lifted Eva high in the air and then let her drop to the water with a big splash, immediately fishing her out and hugging her while they both laughed. Nyssa demanded the same treatment and when she hit the water, she squealed. Savannah's heart tripped.

Her daughters already loved him. They didn't just want a father figure; they wanted Leiandros. And unlike their real father, Leiandros responded to them with all the warmth and approval most Greek males found so easy to give to small children. Both Eva and Nyssa reveled in the open affection.

She couldn't blame them. She yearned for his touch as well, though on a very different level. She wanted his body joined with hers in the primeval act of love. He wanted her too. His arousal had been more than evident the night before. A big part of her mindless reaction had stemmed from the heady knowledge Leiandros could desire her so uncontrollably.

Their need was definitely mutual, but where hers stemmed from strong emotion, she couldn't help wondering if his was connected to his passionate thirst for revenge, or justice as he called it. She sighed, rubbing more sunscreen on her legs. She wasn't even sure she could satisfy him when it came down to consummating their relationship.

Dion had said she was frigid and even after the intimacy she'd already shared with Leiandros, she still half believed Dion. After all, she'd never been able to summon so much as a penny's worth of enthusiasm toward his amorous overtures. On the other hand, one touch from Leiandros and she went up in flames. She pondered the implication of her body's differing reaction to the two men and her mind shied away from acknowledging the reason behind it.

Yet, there were no more barriers now to her attraction to Leiandros, no more reasons to hide her feelings for him, except the fear those feelings would never be returned. Fear she would not measure up in the bedroom. Fear that once he'd had her, he would grow tired of her. Fear that she could not give him the baby son he craved.

The litany of worries running through her mind disgusted her. When had she become such a craven coward?

Watching her daughters bravely take plunge after plunge into the crystal clear waters of the odd shaped pool, something inside of Savannah snapped. *She'd spent four years of her life living under the shadow of fear.*

Hadn't she stayed married to Dion long after she wanted to because she feared he would take away her daughters? She had avoided any semblance of intimacy with a man because she'd been terrified where it might lead. She'd hesitated to bring the girls to Greece because she dreaded their grandparents' reaction to them. If she were being honest with herself, she'd also have to admit that she had been anxious about returning to Greece because of the strong feelings Leiandros invoked in her.

A pathetic creature, holed up in her own little world, letting no one else in for fear they would hurt her, she was even afraid to give those feelings a name.

Her attention returned to Leiandros. If she refused to marry him, would he really refuse her the money to continue her aunt's care? Her instincts told her no, but she couldn't rely on them. They'd also told her to marry a young Greek playboy when she was a very innocent twenty. She had no doubts whatsoever that Leiandros would follow through on his threats regarding the girls. Family was too important to him to allow her to take them back to America, but as she'd told him the day before, she did not have to marry him to remain in Greece.

Eva made another splash, this time the result of diving from Leiandros's steady arms.

Savannah swallowed against a torrent of emotion welling within her. She had two options. Remain safe in her protected little world, or let Leiandros in and take a risk on marrying the man she loved.

Loved. Craved. Needed. Her feelings for him were so strong, it was no wonder she'd tried to sublimate them for seven long years. It hadn't worked. They'd come out in erotic dreams that tortured her sleeping hours. They'd come out in her capitulation about returning to Greece. She could have stayed in Georgia. She'd learned to cope at an early age with the curves life had a tendency to throw at her. No. She'd given up fighting Leiandros because that was what she had *wanted* to do.

Could she go back to her tiny house and lonely bed in Atlanta, even if by some miracle Leiandros allowed it? Her heart beat a steady negative. She loved Leiandros and the thought of losing him was worse than any other fear she'd ever experienced. It was a paralyzing terror. Marriage to a man who did not love her was a risk, but she made a discovery as she lay there soaking in the warmth from the Greek sun.

One emotion overcame fear, making her anxieties about the future seem insignificant. That emotion was love.

She would not give up a future with Leiandros because she feared what it might bring. She loved him and he wanted her. Badly. She would take any bet that he loved her daughters and he wanted *her* to have his babies.

She could build on such a foundation. She *would* build on it. Love would be the cornerstone of her new life, not fear.

CHAPTER TEN

"WHAT conditions?" Leiandros demanded, anger at the intense feeling of relief Savannah's surrender had evoked making his voice harsh.

She stepped back at his tone and her eyes widened before she narrowed them and tilted her elegant chin at an angle. "I need your assurance you will continue to give Eva and Nyssa attention and affection, even after I have your baby."

Offended at the implication he would ignore the precious little girls after the birth of his own child, he bit out, "That goes without saying."

"No, it does not." That stubborn little chin tilted another notch.

Why the hell not? What reason had she to believe he would reject her daughters? "*Eva and Nyssa will be my daughters.* The birth of other children will not negate that truth and as my daughters, they will always have claim to my affection."

She studied him as if weighing his sincerity. Her lack of trust infuriated him, but she finally nodded, her shoulders relaxing. He expected her to continue, but she looked away, her golden brown hair loose for once, falling in a silken mass to shield her expression from him.

"You said a *few* conditions?" he prompted.

Instantly, her entire body went taut with tension.

"Yes." Her pretty hands fisted at her sides. "You must also promise to be faithful."

She dared to demand this of him? "Look at me. I will not discuss this with the back of your head."

She seemed to brace herself and then turned, her face smooth and blank. Her eyes were a different matter. Their green depths had gone dark with some very intense emotion. "Well?"

Did she not realize she had once again questioned his honor? "When we marry, you become my wife, part of me. I would not so dishonor myself or you," he grated, feeling the rein on his temper slip a notch.

She flinched, but gave no sign of backing down. "Not all men consider marriage so binding and let's face it, you don't respect me. I need to know you will respect our marriage enough to compensate for that."

He wanted to kiss that antagonistic expression right off her face. "I have not said I do not respect you."

Her brow rose above challenging green eyes in obvious disbelief. "If you don't consider the numerous insults you have slung at my head testament to your lack of esteem toward me, then I would hate to be on the receiving end of what you do consider disrespectful comments."

"Sarcasm is not an attractive trait in a woman." He had only spoken the truth. His intention had not been to offend or wound her, but clearly he had.

"Evasiveness is even less attractive in a man. Do I have your promise of fidelity, or not?"

He bit back a derisive retort. He was not the partner in this deal that needed watching in this regard. "You have it."

Incredibly her eyes flickered with relief while some of the tenseness went out of her posture.

"I want no other woman, Savannah." He did not know why he offered the reassurance after the way she had insulted him, but needing to touch her, he reached out and pulled her closer to him. "Are there any other conditions?"

He scowled when she nodded again. *What else?*

"I'll marry you. I'll even try to have your baby..." she paused, biting her lip in obvious agitation.

She made the idea of having his child sound like a walk through purgatory. "Don't you want my children?" he demanded, experiencing a totally unaccustomed sense of uncertainty.

Her face suffused with color and she dropped her gaze. "Yes. Yes, I do."

"But?" he asked.

Her hands twisted together in front of her. "What will you do if we only have daughters? Will you divorce me? Or will you expect me to keep having children year after year until I produce your son and heir?"

The picture her words painted appalled him. "I have no intention of divorcing you. Ever. As to heirs...this is not the middle ages. Daughters can inherit as well as sons. I have little trouble seeing Nyssa running Kiriakis International."

Her eyes widened as if he'd shocked her. What did she think? He was some kind of dinosaur? So, perhaps he would prefer a son who shared his character and drive for business, but he would not love daughters any less. Had he not already proven that with Eva and Nyssa?

"Dion wanted sons." The words came out in a whisper he had to strain to hear.

Leiandros tensed at the sound of his cousin's name on Savannah's lips. He did not want to think about Dion being her husband before him, Dion wanting boy babies with her. "It is natural for a man to have this desire, but one cannot dictate the will of God. I want healthy babies and a wife who will love and nurture them as you have done with Eva and Nyssa."

"How many?"

"Be assured I do not wish you to be perpetually pregnant." He wanted a wife as much as he wanted a mother for his children.

Her hands rested against his chest, making it difficult for him to focus on their negotiations. "Give me a number."

A sudden thought occurred to him. "Was pregnancy difficult for you?" Some women struggled with a debilitating morning sickness. Petra hadn't been one of them, so he had not taken such an eventuality into consideration.

Savannah shook her head. "No. I liked being pregnant."

She muttered something under her breath. It sounded like she'd said she liked it when Dion hadn't been around. Leiandros didn't doubt it. A husband tormented by jealousies and the belief his wife carried her lover's child would not have been a pleasant companion or supportive mate during pregnancy.

"Then what is the problem?"

She met his gaze with green eyes filled with resolution. "The problem is gender and what you expect from me if you don't get the son you want to replace the one you lost.''

She wanted a number. Fine. He could give her a number. "Two. I believe raising four children will tax our patience and ingenuity sufficiently, particularly if the younger ones take after Eva and Nyssa.''

He'd meant to make her smile with that last remark and he succeeded. Her eyes twinkled at him. "Well, if they take after their father, I may just put in for early retirement.''

He drew her closer until their bodies were a breath away from touching. "No way. We are in this together, *yineka mou.*''

Whatever she would have said was lost between his lips and hers as he sealed their bargain with a kiss of commitment. She tasted so sweet, it took several seconds before he could lift his mouth from hers. He wanted more, but they were not alone in the house and he had no desire to explain certain matters to his inquisitive soon to be daughters.

"Are there any more conditions?''

To his chagrin, she nodded. "I need to return to Atlanta.''

His hold on her upper arms tightened convulsively. "Absolutely not.'' No way was he letting her leave him like she had left Dion.

She reached out and put her hand on his chest, in an apparent effort to comfort *him.* The touch shouldn't have soothed him, but it did. "I need to go back to take care of Aunt Beatrice. She won't last much longer.'' Pain reflected in her eyes and the downturn of her pretty mouth.

He moved his hands to cup both sides of her face, accepting her pain, even understanding it, but unwilling to be moved by it. "No." This was not negotiable.

She tried to pull away. "I *have* to go back, Leiandros."

He caught her mouth and kissed her lips softly. "No."

"You're being unreasonable."

"I'm being cautious. What good will marriage do me if you insist on staying in Atlanta? Dion learned that lesson the hard way. I refuse to be so trusting."

Her face drained of color, her eyes wounded. "It wasn't the same thing. I *had* to leave Dion. *I don't want to leave you,* but my aunt needs me."

"You can return after our honeymoon."

Her expression lightened to one of relief.

"But you must leave the girls here."

"Impossible!" She tore herself from his hold.

Her angry reaction had an immediate effect on the fit of his chinos. Her passion in any form wreaked havoc with his libido.

"I don't know how long I'll be gone! The girls *can't* stay here." She made an obvious bid to collect herself. *"Please."*

He didn't want her to beg. He wanted her to stay. "They will be my daughters too and I will care for them."

She shook her head wildly. "No. They must go with me."

"We've been through this before. You will not take them out of the country. Accept it."

She deflated like a parachute once the skydiver has landed, her stance one of defeat. "It won't work."

He agreed. Being apart was out of the question. She had to see that. According to the doctors, her aunt did not even recognize Savannah from one day to the next. Why was she so intent on returning to Atlanta to care for the other woman, or was it an excuse to get herself and the girls out of Greece?

"I can't marry you," she said baldly, her eyes filling with tears while a sense of dread caught hold of him.

"*Like hell.* You already gave your word. I won't allow you to change your mind."

"I said there were conditions." She blinked the tears away, rubbing the moisture under her eyes with her fingers.

He felt like cursing. She looked so vulnerable. And the worst of it was: he did not think she was attempting to gain his sympathy. She was trying too hard *not* to give into the tears.

"We can compromise." The very idea was alien to him. He did not usually approve or have need of the concept.

"Your compromises don't work for me." Her voice trembled.

He ignored that declaration. "I have spoken to the doctor in charge of your aunt's care. He says there is one nurse on staff that is a favorite of your aunt's. I can assure she is available for your aunt's personal care."

"I know who you are talking about and she's just discovered she's pregnant. What about when she goes on maternity leave? Will you allow me to go then?"

"According to her doctors, by then your aunt will no longer be with us." His own frustration came out in the cruel statement that he regretted the moment it left his lips.

Savannah did not look beaten any longer. She looked angry enough to attack him. "She is very special to me. She's the only family I've got."

"Do you discount me, my mother, Sandros, Helena and Iona so easily? Even your own daughters? Are we not all your family?"

"That is not what I meant." Some of the anger drained out of her. "She is *my* family. The closest thing to a loving mother that I've ever known."

"You are a Kiriakis." She had married into his family, made lifelong ties that could not be dismissed.

"I love her, Leiandros. I can't let her die alone."

The plea touched him when he wanted to remain unaffected. "According to her doctors, her condition is stable."

"At the moment," she agreed. "How did you know?"

"I call Brenthaven each day." Savannah was his, so her responsibilities were his also.

Her eyes widened and her pale face took on some much needed color. "You call Brenthaven every day?"

"Yes."

She took several seconds to digest this. "I want to go to her if her condition worsens. And even if it doesn't I want to visit her."

"Make them short visits and leave the girls here."

Savannah grimaced, but nodded. "And if she worsens?"

"We will deal with that when it comes, *pethi mou.*"

He could not resist touching her any longer. Pulling

her into his arms, he kissed her. Strangely the feeling coursing through him was not passion, but unexpected tenderness and the light caress of her mouth against his once again soothed him when he least expected to be soothed.

He pulled his head away and rubbed her back. "Okay?"

She shuddered. "Yes."

This time he did not even try to stifle the feeling of relief washing over him like the Mediterranean at high tide.

Savannah waited nervously the next afternoon for the family to gather in the small reception room. Baptista had declared it more intimate, but to Savannah's eyes, it still looked big enough to swallow up most of her small house in Georgia. Leiandros intended to announce their upcoming marriage when everyone was together. Savannah was still trying to deal with her doubts, but accepted she had no real choice.

She loved her aunt too much to allow her to be moved to a state nursing home for the final weeks of her life and she loved Leiandros too much to let him go at all.

He caught her eye as he crossed the room to where she sat on the small settee near the window. He settled next to her, putting his arm casually around her waist and pulling her even closer than the small confines of the settee required. "Are you ready for the announcement?"

Was she? Focusing her attention on Eva and Nyssa sitting on either side of Helena and chattering a mile a minute she accepted the inevitable. "Yes." She could only hope the family responded more warmly to news of her marriage to Leiandros than they had when she married Dion.

Eva and Nyssa had taken to Dion's family with the exuberant affection of the young. They also adored their *honorary* grandmother, Baptista, who would be their real grandmother in less than a week's time.

Leiandros squeezed her and she turned to take in his sculpted features and the enigmatic dark chocolate gaze that made her heart flutter even in a room full of company. "They will all accept you as my wife."

"I hope so."

"They would not dare do otherwise."

She found herself grinning at his arrogance. "Of course not." Then she dropped her gaze in fear her love was shining a little too brightly in her eyes. Now that she'd acknowledged it, she discovered keeping her feelings from Leiandros was difficult indeed.

After everyone was seated, he stood and commanded their attention. Inevitably, he got it. Even her daughters sat perfectly still, their sweet faces turned toward him.

"Today heralds a new beginning for the Kiriakis family. Savannah has returned to us, bringing her daughters to renew relationships with the rest of their family."

Helena nodded, her eyes filled with tears. Baptista smiled approvingly at Savannah while both Sandros and Iona concurred with a Greek gesture of both joy and agreement.

Savannah felt her heart constrict at the obvious acceptance. Leiandros offered her far more than merely himself with marriage. He offered Savannah what she had always craved, had hoped to find with her first marriage, but it had been denied her...a family for herself and now for her daughters.

He nodded his proud head in an arrogant gesture, acknowledging the other's acceptance. "The only improvement which could be made on this new beginning would be for Savannah to once again join our family officially."

The air in the room crackled with expectancy.

Leiandros smiled down at Savannah and she returned the gesture, wondering if this was all just an act for the family's benefit. He wouldn't want them to know he had blackmailed her.

He returned his gaze to the family. "Do you not all agree?" he asked the room in general.

Every head nodded, except the girls who were looking perplexed.

"Then you will congratulate me on convincing Savannah to accept my proposal of marriage."

Pandemonium broke loose. The girls knew what it meant to get married and they jumped up from their seats like two tightly wound springs. Rushing across the room to throw themselves at Leiandros and Savannah, they squealed with delight.

"Does this mean you get to be my true daddy?" Eva asked, as he lifted her high in his arms.

Leiandros hugged her tightly and whispered something in her ear, which made her giggle and glow with happiness.

"Are you really going to marry *Theios?*" Nyssa demanded of Savannah, having crawled right into her lap.

Feeling overwhelmed with emotion, Savannah could only nod and smile, her lips wobbly. Nyssa squealed again and begged to be picked up by Leiandros as well. He stood there, six feet, four inches, of incredible male, holding one of her daughters in each arm and Savannah's heart swelled with so much love for all three of them that she thought it would burst.

Sandros came over and kissed Savannah's cheek before clapping Leiandros on the back. "I thought something like this was in the wind when we went to dinner." He grinned at the others. "Leiandros kept her so close to his side, the poor girl couldn't so much as take a breath and call it her own."

General laughter greeted Sandros's teasing.

As the laughter died, Leiandros set both girls down beside him and drew Savannah to her feet. "It is our custom to exchange rings upon announcing the intent to marry."

An expectant hush fell over the room. Savannah could not speak. He lifted her hand and slipped a ring with a large, deeply green, square cut emerald nestled between two clusters of diamond baguettes onto her finger. He brought her hand to his mouth and brushed his lips over the ring and her skin. His expression burned with possessiveness and she felt heat shooting up her arm from where the ring rested.

Then he slipped a ring into the center of her palm.

She looked down at it. Masculine and heavy, its recessed setting also bore an emerald along with two square cut smaller diamonds on either side. She trembled as she realized that he wanted her to put the ring on his finger, to announce before his family her intention to marry him.

Lifting his hand, she repeated his actions, including

the kiss. Afterward he announced that dinner would be the traditional betrothal feast and the room erupted into applause.

Baptista insisted on kissing and hugging each one of them. She kissed both of Savannah's cheeks. "I'm very pleased."

After many more congratulations, hugs and kisses, someone asked when the wedding was to take place.

"This Sunday," Leiandros replied.

"But that is only three days away!" Baptista cried. "There are so many things to be done, they cannot possibly be accomplished in so short a time."

"It is handled."

Evidently Leiandros's arrogance had no truck with his mother, because Baptista crossed her arms over her small bosom and gave him a glower worthy of an angry sailor. "Bah. What is everything? You could not have invited many guests and kept it such a secret. Do you wish to give your bride the impression you are ashamed of her?"

The haze of happiness surrounding Savannah melted and she shot a quick, questioning glance at Leiandros.

Was he ashamed of her?

His eyes narrowed and he took the two steps separating them before pulling her against his side. "Don't."

That was all he said, but she got the message. Don't worry. Don't doubt him. Don't be afraid, but how could she help it? He was marrying her for revenge and she was hoping it would turn into love. Heavens above! It was one thing to refuse to live a life constricted by fear, another entirely to be an incautious fool. Had she made an awful mistake?

"I am not ashamed of Savannah, but neither do I wish to wait to make her mine in every way."

Sandros laughed while Iona blushed, but Baptista's aggressive stance did not alter. Savannah tried to breathe while feeling like all the air in the room had gone on holiday, her cheeks burning with embarrassment at Leiandros's blatancy.

"You are no adolescent unable to control raging hormones. You are a man, my son. You can wait a few weeks. Your bride deserves to look back at her wedding with fond memories, not regret." Baptista's eyes dared her son to disagree.

His arm tightened around Savannah. "One week from Sunday. That gives you ten days to add whatever touches you and Savannah deem necessary to the wedding, but I will not wait one day longer."

Somehow, his implacability comforted her stressed nerves. He wanted to marry her, but he was willing to wait an extra week to make sure it was a wedding to be proud of. That did not indicate a man ashamed of his chosen bride.

Baptista agreed reluctantly and then launched immediately into plans for the next ten days. Helena and Iona offered their suggestions while Eva and Nyssa repeatedly proclaimed it had to be just like Cinderella in their mama's story.

The following days passed in a blur of activity, leaving Savannah dazed.

Baptista held the opinion that a mere man could know nothing of planning a proper wedding. She insisted on checking each one of her son's plans as well as taking

Savannah all over the island and to Athens in the helicopter for numerous shopping expeditions and lessons in traditional Greek dance. Baptista wanted Savannah to be able to perform the handkerchief dance to start at the reception.

Savannah saw little of Leiandros during these hectic days leading up to the wedding. Though he came home every evening from his office at Kiriakis International to spend time with her and the girls, he disappeared into his study to work after tucking them into bed. He said he needed to catch up on recently neglected work and clean his desk for their upcoming weeklong honeymoon.

She hadn't wanted to be parted for the girls for any longer and much to her surprise, he had acceded to her wishes. Even more surprising was the evident effort he had put into providing her with a dream wedding, effort he had to have expended before she had even come to Greece.

As the days progressed Savannah decided Leiandros was no ordinary man, because he knew quite a lot about weddings. The wedding gown he had chosen was declared fit for a princess. When she donned the simple veil, Baptista and the seamstress she had hired to make last minute alterations clapped their hands in approval.

He had brought in her favorite Southern magnolias along with fragrant gardenias to be mixed with traditional Greek flowers for her bouquet in one of the many efforts he had made to mix her customs with his. He had also taken an active interest in the expanded guest list, making sure they invited enough relations, friends and important business associates to fill the chapel and Villa Kalosorisma for the reception.

As each item fell into place and the wedding drew nearer, rather than bridal nerves, Savannah experienced a growing anticipation at the thought of linking her life with Leiandros.

She woke well before the maid came to deliver her breakfast on the day of her wedding. Baptista arrived with Eva and Nyssa in tow as Savannah was drinking her coffee. Baptista opened the terrace doors and the sound of aoud and fiddle music playing accompaniment to a male singer drifted in.

"What is that?" Eva asked as she climbed to sit on the bed next to Savannah. Nyssa was soon snuggled up to her other side.

"The music for dressing," Baptista replied. "It is tradition. The bridegroom arranges this treat for his bride."

Savannah warmed at Baptista's words and the rest of the morning was filled with happy chatter as the women prepared for the wedding in Savannah's room. A stylist came in and did everyone's hair and makeup. All too soon, it was time for Savannah to put on her wedding gown. As she slipped into the antique white satin, she felt like the princess her daughters kept calling her.

Someone knocked on the door and Baptista opened it.

"It is time," Savannah heard from the cracked doorway.

From then on, everything happened in a blur. A large group of wedding guests waited outside the villa's main entrance to join the procession to the chapel. Savannah sought Leiandros's commanding presence and her heart settled in her chest when she saw him. Dressed in morning coat with tails, he looked like the prince to her very own fairy tale.

They stopped outside the chapel in order for the priest to bless the rings before he led them inside.

The wedding itself was more like a church service, though the priest stopped to lead them in the traditional vows Savannah was accustomed to. Baptista had told her that Greek weddings rarely included vows as they were the union of two souls rather than a contract. Regardless of the reasoning, Savannah's heart rejoiced as Leiandros looked deeply into her eyes and promised to forsake all others.

He had done this for her and she smiled tremulously, her voice shaking as she promised to love and honor him.

When she saw the headpieces Leiandros had selected for the crowning, all the air left her lungs in one long gush. They truly were crowns fit for a king and queen, obviously made with real gold or at least overlay and encrusted with precious stones and gems. Several women sighed as the delicate tiara was settled on Savannah's head and the masculine counterpart placed on Leiandros.

They were pronounced man and wife and regardless of Greek custom, Leiandros kissed her with pent up passion and unmistakable possessiveness.

She could almost hear him saying, "You are mine now."

And she was.

CHAPTER ELEVEN

"YOU performed the handkerchief dance very well."

Savannah turned her head and smiled at Iona. They had developed a friendship of sorts, but neither woman mentioned the past or Dion.

"It was fun. Baptista wanted me to be perfect so she took me to lessons. I practiced until my legs felt like noodles and my arms threatened to fall off."

Iona grinned and winked. "Well, you got it right and from the sparks shooting between you and my cousin, Leiandros thought so as well."

Sparks? The feelings Leiandros incited in Savannah were more like a forest fire blazing out of control. Her entire body thrummed with anticipation for the upcoming night. He had done everything in his power to make her that way, too, at least that's how she felt. He'd been touching her constantly all day, nothing overt, a brush here, a caress there, but all of them fed the desire now raging through her blood.

The reception had been going on for what seemed like hours and she did not know how much longer she could wait to be alone with him without exploding on the spot.

"Look…"

Savannah looked where Iona had pointed. The men were gathering in a circle on the area by the pool that had been set aside for dancing.

Iona said, "The men are beginning the traditional dance."

Leiandros stood a head taller than most of the other men, his body rippling with muscles under the white shirt and pants he wore, all that remained of his wedding finery. He faced her across the large patio, his eyes holding hers as the dance began.

Soon, the eye contact was broken, but not Savannah's concentration. She knew peripherally other men were dancing and guests were clapping their hands, shouting their appreciation, but all she saw was him. Her husband. His body could feed the fantasies of the entire female population of Greece. He certainly fulfilled hers. With each turn and kick his muscles bulged against the single layer of fabric covering them.

Her body heated while her mouth went dry with desire. She didn't know how long the men danced before people started throwing plates, but when one was placed in her hand, she threw it down with passionate zeal, all the while her gaze never once moving from Leiandros. She felt powerless against the feelings coursing through her.

One by one, the men dropped out of the dance until Leiandros and two others were all that remained. For the first time since he had started dancing, Leiandros looked at her and she felt her throat constrict.

"Here, child." Was that Baptista's voice?

Enthralled with the movements of the dance and the sheen of sweat covering the V of chest exposed by Leiandros's shirt, Savannah couldn't make herself turn to find out. She took the plate and as Leiandros and the other two men went into a series of fast paced turns and steps, she threw it. It crashed onto the tile two feet in front of Leiandros.

Leiandros's eyebrows rose at the gesture.

She smiled brilliantly at him and took another plate from someone, throwing it to splinter into pieces near the other. The two men dancing with Leiandros moved away and he was the only dancer left, but then he'd been the only dancer in her eyes since the beginning.

She took another plate, this time from Iona, she thought, and tossed it with fervor. It broke directly in front of him. He smiled then, his eyes making sexual promises that made her body tremble. She'd broken three more plates when he started to dance in a pattern leading to her. He stopped when he reached her and she stared.

She could do nothing else.

He bent, placing one arm behind her knees and the other curved around her ribcage, then straightened lifting her high into his arms. The skirts of her dress billowed around them, while the guests yelled their approval and some of the men tossed suggestions to Leiandros that bordered on the risqué.

It all felt like a movie playing around her, muted and remote. The only reality was his hard chest against her side, his hand gripping her ribs, his thumb subtly brushing the side of her breast, the musky scent of his heated body and the promise in his dark as sin eyes.

He turned and shouted something to the guests and then carried her swiftly toward the helo pad. They had said goodbye to the girls earlier, while taking a break from the reception to tuck Eva and Nyssa into their beds.

There was nothing and no one to hinder their departure.

Aboard the helicopter, Savannah didn't even try to talk to Leiandros. The noise of the whirling blades made any sort of discussion impossible. She had expected to ride in the limo to the hotel attached to the restaurant they'd eaten at in Halkida. It took her several minutes to realize they weren't headed for Halkida at all.

She turned to Leiandros and shouted, "Where are we going?"

He smiled mysteriously and shook his head.

They'd been in the helicopter for about twenty-five minutes when she recognized the outskirts of Athens. Ten minutes later, they landed on the rooftop helo pad of a tall building in the business sector. Leiandros jumped out, grabbed her by the waist and lifted her out. Then he led her, running, away from the wind created by the blades.

When they got out of the radius of the blades, he once again swept her into his arms. A man opened a door leading from the roof to the interior of the building and Leiandros moved inside. He carried her down a short flight of steps, through another security door and into a waiting lift.

"Where are we?" she asked, breathless.

"Can you not guess, *yineka mou?*"

She probably could, if her brain could focus on something other than the fascinating play of light on his black hair.

He used the hand under her knees to press in a security code and the lift started moving. It stopped seconds later. The doors slid open and he carried her into a small foyer, keyed another security code outside the door and then pushed it open.

Finally it dawned on her where they were. "We're in your penthouse at the top of the Kiriakis building."

She'd only been here once before—the night of the fateful party. The night she had met him for the first time and allowed him to kiss her into almost complete submission.

Her gaze darted around her, taking in the entry hall and the living room as he carried her inside.

"It all looks the same," she whispered.

He nodded, his expression almost grim. "Petra was not interested in the penthouse. She spent most of her time living in a villa I bought near her parents."

Savannah knew right then and there, she never wanted to step foot in that villa. It belonged to another woman. "She didn't live at Villa Kalosorisma?"

He studied her face, his own expressionless. "Never."

Savannah let out a breath she didn't realize she'd been holding. Fiercely glad that her home was truly hers, she smiled involuntarily.

"You like that?" he asked.

She couldn't deny it. "Yes."

"You're possessive, but then so am I." He swung around and carried her out onto the terrace.

He lowered her to her feet, keeping her body molded to his. She couldn't see his face in the shadowy darkness and felt an atavistic shiver shake her. What was he thinking?

"Do you remember?" he asked, his voice almost harsh.

The kiss. He meant the kiss. "Yes." She had never been able to forget.

"I wanted you that night, Savannah. I was furious to find out you already belonged to another man. My own cousin."

She had sensed his fury at the time, but assumed it was directed at her for responding to him when she was married to Dion. "I belong to you now." He had to know it. He only had to brush against her and she lost touch with reality.

He growled something low in Greek and then he kissed her, just like that fateful night. His mouth moved on hers in tender exploration as if he'd never kissed her before, his tongue coming out to softly trace the outline of her lips. And just like before, she melted, her body going boneless against his. The kiss went on and on. Just like before, but unlike before, when he placed his hands on the outer curves of her breasts, she did not pull away.

She did not have to. He groaned his approval as his hands slid to her back and undid the zip cleverly hidden under a row of tiny buttons and loops. Her breath stopped in her throat as he undid her dress inch by tantalizing inch. Would he never finish? Her feminine flesh ached for him, and she pressed her thighs together, trying to alleviate the almost painful pleasure. It only made it worse.

She was going to expire from need before he even got her dress off.

"Leiandros…" his name came out a plea against his lips.

He hushed her with his mouth, taking possession of

the vulnerable interior of hers with his tongue. And the zip lowered another inch. She didn't feel boneless anymore, she felt desperate and her body squirmed against him, while his hands and tongue tormented her to higher levels of passion.

She loved him so much. She wanted to feel him inside of her, connected to her in the most fundamental way, their bodies joined, their souls one. She didn't care about preliminaries. She needed him now! But he acted like he had all the time in the world and kissed her lazily as he continued lowering that wretched zipper.

She would have screamed in frustration, but her mouth was too busy enjoying his.

Finally, the zipper gave completely and the edges of her dress parted under his expert fingers. Fingers that caressed the now incredibly sensitive skin of her back.

She moaned, wanting him to move those fingers to her front, her swollen breasts craving his touch, their tight peaks aching for his possession. She pressed herself against him, rubbing from side to side, but the friction of her gown only increased her torment.

She wanted the caress of his hands on her, not satin.

He stepped back and she tried to follow him, but he wouldn't let her. He looked down at her. "I burned for you that night, but my body had to go unsatisfied. I tried to drown the ache in another woman."

She didn't like hearing that and knew she had no right to feel that way. "Did it work?" she had to ask.

"She wasn't you." His voice sounded accusing.

Savannah let the bodice of her dress fall, to reveal her unrestricted breasts, her erect nipples jutting forth proudly. "I'm here now."

He swore, but instead of touching her as she expected, he swung her up in his arms and carried her back inside all the way to the master bedroom. When he got there, he dropped her legs and she stood against him, her bare breasts pressed against the silk of his shirt. But still he didn't touch her.

She whimpered her longing.

With another curse, he undressed her with barely suppressed hunger until she stood before him with not one stitch of clothing to hide behind, her body vulnerable to his dark gaze.

He stepped back. "Stay there."

His growled command rooted her to the spot, primal feminine fear curling around the edges of her desire.

He punched a button and recessed lighting illuminated the room. Although mellow, the light made her feel exposed. Still fully dressed, he stood a few feet away and stared at her, letting his eyes move over her body in a way that made her feel like a piece of artwork for sale and he the collector.

She started to lift her hands to cover herself.

"Don't!" he warned and her hands fell back to her sides of their own volition, her body shivering in response to his tone.

"What's happening?" She didn't think this was the sort of seduction most brides experienced on their wedding nights.

He was silent for several seconds before answering. "I wanted you here, like this. That night. I wanted you, naked in my bedroom, on my bed, under me."

His words sent arrows of sensations to her already moist feminine flesh, but his expression did something else entirely. He looked enraged with some kind of male sexual antagonism and tormented. It was the torment that kept her still.

Yet under the oppression of his gaze, she shivered again, the second time in as many minutes. She tried to tell herself she was just tired, that she was imagining the dangerous weight of his look, that he would not hurt her. It had been a wonderful, but emotional day. Perhaps her mind was playing tricks on her.

None of the arguments succeeded in dispelling the gathering sense of doom surrounding her in its shadows, bringing chills to her naked flesh and making her heart beat like that silly little old jackrabbit.

But, she *wasn't* helpless. She was a woman, his woman, his *yineka* and she would not cower to the fear that dogged her like darkness chasing the sunset.

She let her eyes meet his now obsidian gaze.

He showed no expression as she began moving toward him, her heart pounding against her ribs with a combination of apprehension and desire. "Well, I'm *here. In your bedroom.*"

She veered her path as she came into touching distance of him and headed toward the oversized king bed. White gauze draped from the ceiling, the excess folds gathered with gold rope to each of the corners of the four-poster bed.

She climbed onto the high mattress. Kneeling, she faced him. *"On your bed."*

His jaw set in a hard line of uncompromising strength. He said nothing. Nor did he move. His eyes did not flicker.

She sucked in air and let it out again. "If you want

me *under you,* you'll have to take your clothes off and join me.''

She'd never been this bold. Had never wanted to be this wanton, but with this man, she felt no inhibitions. His manner caused small jolts of trepidation to skitter along her nerve endings, but instead of turning her off, she felt more excited, more ready to mate with her chosen lover.

Something was going on in his head, something to do with the night they'd kissed, but she knew with every fiber of her feminine being that Leiandros wanted her.

And he was going to have her, but not as some sorry little sacrifice. She intended to meet him equally, to give pleasure and to take it as well. So, she waited, waited for him to undress, waited for him to come to her.

They faced each other, both aggressors, both unwilling to bend. Until she started taking the pins from her hair. His eyes fixed on the movement of her fingers as strand by silky strand settled against her nape and shoulders, falling to the center of her back. She dropped the pins to the floor, each one landing silently against the thickly piled carpet.

When she finished, she moved to one corner of the bed and untied the gold rope. Two drapes swooshed down. She went to each corner, repeating her actions until the gauze completely enclosed the bed and Leiandros's figure was hazy through the sheer white fabric.

Then she laid down, lifting the leg closest to him, creating a visual barrier to her feminine secrets. In contrast, she stretched her arms above her head, arching her back so her breasts were shown to their best advantage. "Are you coming?"

The untamed sound he made thrilled her and she watched through the gauze as he stripped off his shirt, sending buttons flying all over the room. One landed against the bed curtains and slid to the floor.

He was more careful with his pants, easing the zipper down slowly over his obviously excited male flesh. She had a short glimpse of him standing gloriously proud in only his tiny male briefs before those, too, were dispensed with. She caught her breath at his full nudity.

Heavens, he was big. Her throat constricted with fear again, but this time it was the instinctual fear of a woman faced with her mate's full masculine strength for the first time. She knew her eyes were wide and her mouth parted in wonder as he approached the bed, his movements predatory and determined, but she couldn't help it.

She'd only actually seen male nudity a handful of times. Dion had preferred the dark and he'd never looked like this.

"You're magnificent," she whispered in awe and he faltered as he drew apart the curtains.

Laughter erupted from him as he launched toward her, landing with his huge body covering her, his weight pressing down her drawn up leg. The amusement in his eyes died as their naked bodies touched. She grabbed his head, trying to bring it down to meet her lips.

"You little torment! I hope you're ready for me. After that performance, I want to be inside you." He let her pull his mouth nearer and kissed her, his lips hot, his tongue intrusive. "Now," he said as if she didn't already get the picture.

Then, he grabbed her hands and kept them above her head with one of his, his expression tenderly menacing.

She answered with her body, letting her thighs spread apart and tipping her pelvis toward that magnificent male erection. She'd been ready since the final dance at the reception.

She'd wanted him outside on the terrace so badly she would have let him love her there, but he'd insisted on coming into the bedroom and playing that silly game.

"Take me," she demanded.

And he did. *Heavens,* how he did. For all his macho warnings, he didn't enter her with even a semblance of lust filled violence. He positioned himself against her opening and rocked himself inside her with a sensuous back and forth motion that had her insides swelling against him and her feelings spiraling toward that starburst of pleasure she had felt once before in his arms.

All the while his mouth pressed hot, salacious kisses all over her face down to the sensitive skin behind her ear and he rubbed the black curling hair on his rock hard chest against her oversensitive nipples.

She yanked her hands from his loosened hold and gripped his bottom, pulling him deeper inside with the strength of Samson as she felt the pleasure spin out of control. She heard a scream, followed by a guttural shout that would have deafened her if she hadn't been lost in wave after stupendous wave of mind-numbing pleasure. She floated in the aftermath until her heartbeat slowed and her eyes could focus again.

She smiled at him. "Am I dead?"

His eyes narrowed. *"No."*

"I must be," she teased and leaned up to kiss him. "I'm definitely in Heaven."

His too serious expression lightened to smug satisfaction. "Remember, it's only this *magnificent* male that can take you there. You belong to me now, *yineka mou,* and no one else will ever touch you this way again."

The underlying warning in his voice pricked at her heart. How could he think for one single, solitary second that she could *ever* go to another man's bed after sharing his?

"How did you know?" she asked, tongue in cheek, wanting to dispel the gloom settling over her.

He stilled, his semierect flesh hardening slightly inside her. "What do you mean?"

"I've never felt that way before." She played with the hair on his chest, pressing her fingers against the muscles underneath, their hardness attesting to his physical strength. She absolutely reveled in her freedom to touch him. "Well, except that time on the terrace. Couldn't you tell?"

"Never?" he demanded, sounding incredulous.

"Never," she repeated. "It was never you before."

He deserved that admission after the one he'd made on the terrace. His nearly black eyes burned into her, while his flesh went fully erect in the space of a heartbeat.

"Oh," she exclaimed. "Again? So soon?"

But he was too busy moving and touching every pleasure spot she knew of on her body and some she'd never suspected she possessed to answer.

Hours and repeated bouts of lovemaking later, he laid

with his head resting on her breast, his hand lazily moving over her skin, touching, branding, *knowing* her.

She tried to stifle a yawn, but couldn't quite accomplish the feat.

His head came up, his expression smug. "Tired, *moro mou?*"

Wanting to touch him some more, but too beat to move, she said, "Yes."

"That's too bad," he said in a voice that made her pulse leap, as spent as her body was.

"Is it?" she asked, her mind occupied with the way his fingers felt against her most sensitive flesh.

"Much, much too bad."

"Why?" she asked, her breath hitching in her throat.

"Because I haven't done everything I wanted to do yet."

There was *more?* "Like what?"

He kissed her nipple, teasing it with the tip of his tongue. "Like this." And his lips closed over the tender bud as he began a strong sucking motion that had her moaning.

Incredibly, he was right. He'd touched every inch of her flesh, licked most of it and nipped certain highly sensitive areas, but he hadn't once done this, the expected.

"I guess that means I don't get to go to sleep yet," she said, trying to sound disappointed, but failing miserably.

She couldn't have gone to sleep now for all the peaches in Georgia. She slid her hand onto his chest, finding the male counterpart of the flesh he was pleasuring so thoroughly, and lightly rubbed it. He arched against her hand and she made little circles around his flat male nipple before gently pinching it between her thumb and forefinger.

He nearly came off the bed. "Yes. Little torment. Just like that. Don't stop."

And she didn't.

They fell asleep, sweaty, sated and curled in one another's arms as the Greek sun started to rise, pouring diffused amber light through the gauze covered master bedroom's huge window.

CHAPTER TWELVE

"WAKE up, *yineka mou*. It is time to get up."

Leiandros's voice filtered through the layers of sleep fogging Savannah's brain.

"Why?" she muttered, not bothering to lift her head from the pillow. Her body ached in places she'd never recognized as having muscles and her eyes felt filled with sand.

"Come, *agapi mou*. Open your eyes."

Her eyes flew wide and she sat straight up, the white sheet falling around her waist. Had he just called her his love? She searched his face, but didn't see any sign of tenderness.

His eyes were serious, his mouth grim and the set of his shoulders stiff. "You must be strong."

Panic welled up in her chest. "Eva? Nyssa? My babies?"

"Are fine." He reached out and placed a warm hand on her bare shoulder. "It is your aunt."

Savannah could not make herself ask the question that needed to be asked.

He seemed to sense her hesitation and answered as if she'd voiced the words. "She is alive, but she has had another stroke. The doctor does not expect her to recover."

Savannah sagged against the pillows. "What do you mean?" Her words came out in an agonized whisper because she knew what he meant. Aunt Beatrice was going to die. "How long?"

"They do not know. Maybe a day, maybe a week."

"I need to go." She tensed for his refusal.

"The jet is at the airport as we speak. The helicopter is on the roof waiting to take us there. Take a shower and dress. You can eat on the plane. I've already packed for us."

"You're going with me? You're letting me go?" She couldn't take it in.

"Of course." He shrugged. "You are my wife. Your concerns are my concerns."

His words shocked her so much, she was in the shower when she thought of the girls.

Dressed in the clothes he had provided, her hair still damp, she left the bathroom in search of Leiandros. She ran him down in the study. He was on the phone.

When he saw her enter, he cut the call immediately and turned to face her. "Ready?"

"What about the girls?" She couldn't think, didn't know what to do.

"They are content with their grandmothers. The girls expect us to be gone a week. There is no reason to upset them with the news."

She nodded. She'd taken them to visit Aunt Beatrice only rarely because having the children around upset the older woman and therefore upset the girls as well. They had already said their goodbyes.

"I'm ready." She fingered the lightweight red fabric of her ankle length sleeveless dress. "This is very comfortable."

His smile was wry. "I admit comfort was not high on my list when I chose it."

The way he was looking at how the dress clung to her curves made her blush. "Oh. You picked it out?" Remembering his reaction to her dress the night they'd almost made love in his car, she thought she knew why he'd chosen this particular color.

"Yes." He didn't add anything else, but led her from the apartment back into the lift they had ridden the night before.

Leiandros insisted she try to sleep on the plane. She had no success until he joined her on the bed, pulling her tightly into the curve of his body and soothing her with his presence. They reached Atlanta in just over eight hours. When she expressed her surprise at the swift flight, he informed her that he'd had the pilot fly at the maximum speed allowed for the new jet without having to stop along the way for refueling.

Once again Leiandros had arranged VIP treatment through customs and had a limousine waiting for them at the airport to take them directly to Brenthaven. He kept her close to his side during the journey and her hand latched to his own as they walked down the quiet corridors of Brenthaven.

The room smelled like a hospital and Aunt Beatrice lay against the pillows, her translucent skin the color of the sheets. Savannah approached the bed, listening to the labored breathing of the woman in a coma lying there. Starting to shake, Savannah tried to stifle the pain filled moan that crawled up her throat.

She could no longer pretend to herself that one day Aunt Beatrice would come back to her.

Suddenly, Leiandros's arm was there, wrapped around her trembling shoulders. "Tell me about her."

So she did, through the interminable hours that followed she told him about her aunt, how she had raised a little girl orphaned by her mother's death and her father's desertion. Savannah shared the terror she'd experienced when her aunt was diagnosed with Alzheimer's when Savannah was nineteen, her desperation when near disaster had forced Savannah to put her aunt in a public nursing home.

"You married Dion so you could move your aunt here."

She didn't want to talk about her former marriage, so she just shrugged. "Nothing's quite that simple."

He didn't pursue it, but maintained his place beside her, ordering in food when he determined she should be hungry, cajoling her into drinking fruit juices when she'd have settled for black coffee and listening to her talk whenever she needed to. Ten hours later, her aunt quietly slipped away, never having regained consciousness.

Savannah's eyes remained dry as she listened to Leiandros make arrangements with the doctor. Her stoic expression did not waver when he led her from Brenthaven to the waiting limo, but when they got inside, he pulled her onto his lap and her defenses collapsed.

She burrowed into his chest, seeking a hiding place from her pain. She felt tears well and for the first time in almost two decades, she let them fall unrestrained.

Leiandros tightened his hold on her. "Cry, *pethi mou*. Let the grief out."

And she did. She cried out her grief over being alone in the world for so long. She finally mourned the lost years of her marriage, the pain of Dion's betrayal and Leiandros's contempt. But most of all, she wept for the woman who had been the closest thing to a real mother Savannah had ever had.

Through it all, he held her. When they reached her modest little house, he carried her inside while she continued to soak his shoulder and the front of his shirt.

"Our room?" he asked, implying his ownership of both her and her home.

She pointed down the hall.

He carried her through the bedroom into her private bath. She clung to him as he turned on the shower and began undressing them both. They were under the hot spray of water before her tears finally shuddered to a halt. She wrapped her arms around his waist and pressed herself against the warmth of his body. Even in the hot shower, she felt cold.

"She loved me when no one else would. I'm alone now."

He put his hands on her shoulders and pushed her far enough away that he could look into her face. "You are *not* alone. You are mine."

How could such possessive words sound so good to her battered soul?

After that, he remained silent, washing them both, then taking her out of the shower and toweling her dry like a baby.

"Go lie down. I'll get you a glass of water."

She obeyed without a murmur. She had climbed naked between the sheets, when he returned to the room with a tray. A carafe of chilled water, two glasses and two fresh peaches, sliced and peeled looked very enticing on the tray.

"Where did those come from?" She pointed to the peaches.

"I had the kitchen stocked and the house opened and aired while we were on our way here."

He had thought of everything. After drinking her water, she sat docile while he tenderly hand fed her peach slices. As he continued to feed her the mood around them subtly changed and he lingered over her lips with a gentle touch as she drew out every bite. She didn't know when her melancholy turned to desire, but soon she was feeding him succulent, slippery slices of peach, dipping her fingertips into his mouth with the fruit and sucking on his fingers when he returned the favor.

He shuddered. "Savannah?"

"I need you." So simple. So true. She needed assurance that she belonged to him, that she was not alone.

He placed the tray on the floor and then tumbled her back against the pillows, devouring her lips with his own. Though their kisses were passionate, hot and uncontrolled, at the first touch of his male flesh against her femininity, something in him changed. He took her with so much tenderness, so much gentle wooing, more tears seeped from her eyes, but there was no sadness in them.

She felt reborn by his touch and when the final pleasure came, it rolled over her in inexhaustible waves and still he did not stop. He continued to move in her and on her, kissing her eyelids, sipping her tears of passion and nuzzling her.

He carefully built the passion in her to a new crescendo, but this time when the cymbals crashed, he was with her. He did not withdraw for a long time and she did not want him to. This oneness was like an oasis to her thirsty soul.

When he finally moved out of her, he pulled her close to his side and kissed her temple. "You are not alone. I am with you, *yineka mou.*"

And he was. Through the funeral service, through the packing of her and the girls remaining personal possessions and in bed. Most definitely in bed. She slept cuddled to his body every night after making love and with each passing day her love for him grew and grew until she realized it had no bounds and exulted in the knowledge.

The night before they were to return to Greece, Savannah insisted on cooking, though Leiandros had hired a temporary daily cook and cleaner to make things easier for her. After they finished eating, she led him into the living room for coffee. She set the tray on the coffee table in front of the couch and poured the steaming brew into mugs before taking a seat beside Leiandros in the center of the sofa.

He took a sip of his coffee, his sensual lips pressing against the ceramic mug. "Your coffee is excellent, *pethi mou,* but I will be happy to drink Greek coffee again."

Not in the least offended, she smiled. Coffee didn't

really interest her right now, but then very little could compete with him.

She put her mug down and snuggled into his side. Would she ever grow accustomed to this freedom to draw comfort from his body whenever she wanted it? "I'm going to miss this house."

It had been a true refuge after the annihilation of her marriage.

He cupped her nape with long masculine fingers, letting his thumb rub a soothing pattern just below her ear. "Are you sorry to be returning to Greece?"

Her head popped up and she looked into dark chocolate eyes that shielded his secrets. "How can you ask that?" Couldn't he tell how much she needed him now? She'd never worked up the courage to tell him she loved him, but he had to know it.

He shrugged and pressed her head back to rest against his chest. "It does not matter. You belong to me now."

She smiled at his arrogance. "And you belong to me."

He didn't answer, but he did not deny it, either.

They finished their coffee, discussing last minute details of her permanent return to Greece, but Leiandros grew increasingly quiet until the conversation stopped altogether.

He drew away from her and looked at her with eyes that had gone black with some unnamed emotion. "Tell me about the lover that hurt you."

Bewildered by this totally unexpected change in topic, she asked, "What are you talking about?"

Then the full impact of his words hit her. He still believed she had taken lovers during her first marriage.

After the emotional and physical intimacy they had shared, she could not accept his clinging to such a belief. She had meant to tell him the truth, but somehow with all that he had done for her since the wedding, she'd come to believe it was unnecessary.

Obviously, she'd been wrong and their intimacy meant nothing in the face of his old resentments.

He took her hand in his, in what she assumed was supposed to be a comforting gesture, but she was too furious to feel anything but her anger. "There is no need to evade the subject. I know someone hurt you. You shied away from me when you first arrived in Greece. You are still uncomfortable in close proximity to other men, even Sandros."

Actually, she thought she'd done rather well at their wedding reception, giving and receiving numerous hugs and kisses of congratulations on her cheeks from one man after another as well as the women.

"And you believe one of my *many* lovers hurt me?" she asked, her voice scathing, her heart hurting.

His mouth tautened into a grim line. "Are you trying to convince me it did not happen? There is no need."

She sprang up from the couch, her body prickling with enraged tension. *"Damn you, Leiandros. Are you truly that blind?"* she shrieked at him.

His eyes widened in shock. "Do not swear at me."

She glared at Leiandros, her fury so great she had to take a deep breath before she could get the words out she wanted to say. "I can swear any damn time I want to!"

When he opened his mouth to speak, she rushed on, her voice loud enough to drown out anything he might utter. "Where is your evidence of my infidelity?" She swung her arms wide in a gesture of disbelief. *"Where?"*

He remained silent, his expression giving nothing away.

"That's right. You have none! You have only your cousin's word and he lied about me with horrific regularity. You accept that my daughters are Kiriakises. What chance is there if I were so promiscuous they would both be his?"

She inhaled another deep breath and went on. "Did you ever see me flirt? Did you ever see me make eyes at other men? Your investigator told you I hadn't dated in the last three years. What makes you think I was any different before?"

"The kiss." Just that. No more words.

She was so mad she wanted to spit, something a Southern lady was never to do. "Who pulled away first, Leiandros?" she demanded. "Who told you I was married? *Me!* Yes, I responded, but I didn't lead you on. I did not invite that kiss and after it happened, what did I do? I avoided you, to the point of ignoring instincts for my own safety."

"Explain that last remark," he barked at her, his unemotional façade cracking.

"You bet I'll explain. You just wait right there."

She whirled from the room, stormed into her tiny study, opened the safe and pulled out a large manila envelope.

She stomped back into the living room and threw the envelope on the coffee table in front of Leiandros. "Your answers are in there. Open it."

*   *   *

Savannah sat at the old-fashioned vanity, brushing the remaining dampness from her hair when Leiandros came into the room. She must have taken a shower. She'd wrapped her black velvet robe around her irresistible nakedness and tied the waist with a big knot.

He sighed. Her nonverbal communication was clear. *Don't touch.* But then he could not blame her. His stomach churned with nausea at what he had read and seen. Their eyes met in the mirror, hers still simmering with fury.

She didn't stop brushing her hair. "I suppose you've convinced yourself I deserved it, being such an immoral slut and all."

"*Theos mou.* Don't!" His voice was harsh with emotion. He could not stand the implication he could ever condone such a thing. He held the pictures toward her. "How many times did this happen before you left him?"

She put the brush down, but continued to face the mirror. "What difference does it make?"

"*How many?*"

"Once," she said defiantly.

What did she think? He would have expected her to stick around for more of the same?

"Tell me." He needed to know.

She spun to face him, her eyes burning accusation at him, but worse was the stark pain clouding their green depths. "Why? You think you know the story already. According to you, I was some kind of bed-hopping bimbo when I was married to your cousin. Obviously he got fed up and lost his temper."

Even if that were the case, there was no excuse for

what Dion had done to her. "Tell me the truth. Tell me how it really was," he practically begged.

Her eyes mirrored wariness. "Will you believe me?"

He no longer knew what to believe about his cousin's marriage to Savannah. The picture Dion had painted of her did not coincide with the woman Leiandros had come to know since her return to Greece.

This woman cared deeply for her children, reacted generously toward people who had hurt her in the past and had taken on responsibility for an elderly woman's care when she was barely old enough to be on her own.

His silence condemned him and before he could rectify the situation, she jumped up from the vanity chair.

"When you figure it out, let me know. Then *I'll* decide whether or not I want to tell you." She stalked over to the bed and grabbed one of the pillows, then opened the cedar chest at its foot, taking out a quilt and turned to leave the room.

Panic slammed through him, his superior brain not working for once. "Where are you going?"

She fixed him with that blank-eyed stare that said she was keeping her emotions under wraps. "I think I'll sleep on the couch tonight."

He said the first thing that came to mind. "Do not think you can manipulate me by withholding your body." As soon as the words left his mouth, he knew they were the wrong ones.

Not so much as a single facial muscle moved in the blank mask of her face. "I would not begin to dream that I could. In fact, I've finally wised up enough to stop dreaming completely."

And then she was gone, while he stood motionless

calling himself every kind of fool and a few words he would never use in her company.

Savannah lay on the couch, dry-eyed and hurting so much it was hard to breathe. She'd come to the couch instinctively for comfort. It was one of the few pieces of furniture she'd kept in storage when she moved to Greece the first time. She'd slept on this same sofa for the first year she had lived with Aunt Beatrice, but the comfort she sought wasn't there.

Leiandros did not believe her. She had bared her soul, showing him the pictures of her bruised body, her copy of the doctor's report and the restraining order. And he still believed his cousin had been the saint.

Her fists twined together, clenching the quilt as if it were a lifeline, but there was no lifeline. Her dreams were in ashes and her love mangled beyond recognition.

He'd demanded she tell him the truth, but what he'd meant was her version of it. He'd retained the right to judge the merit and honesty of her words. She bit her bottom lip in an attempt to stifle the sobs demanding release from her breast until she tasted blood. She'd thought she could live with a one-sided love, that she would eventually overcome his prejudices and mistrust.

She accepted now she never would.

If he could still believe Dion had been the victim after seeing those pictures, there was no hope for her future with Leiandros. His blindness toward his cousin's true nature would always stand between them. She could ask Sandros to tell Leiandros the truth, but to what purpose? He didn't trust *her* and she couldn't live with that distrust.

A low moan of pain escaped her slightly parted lips and she curled into a fetal ball, her hands still clenched in the quilt.

A warm, slightly trembling masculine hand covered her clenched ones, and another hand cupped her cheek. "I'm sorry, baby. I'm so sorry, *moro mou.*"

Startled, she opened her eyes to see the shadowed contours of his face and his glorious, naked body kneeling beside the couch.

"Come to bed, *yineka mou.*" His husky voice sounded strangely pleading.

But she shook her head in denial. "I don't want to sleep with you."

She thought she detected red scorching his sculpted cheekbones in the dim light, but decided she was being fanciful. Leiandros Kiriakis was not capable of a vulnerable reaction like blushing.

"If you mean make love, I won't try to seduce you." He paused as if he found it difficult to get the next words out. "I only want to hold you. I *need* to hold you."

Need? He didn't need anyone, least of all her. She was just his "instrument of justice," the means by which he could have his precious heir and bring Eva and Nyssa back into the Kiriakis fold. "*Right.* Go to bed, Leiandros. It's late. We need our rest."

"But I cannot rest, not after my idiocy earlier."

Did he expect her mercy when he had given her none? She closed her eyes, blocking out the temptation of his body and the look of pleading in his eyes. It was probably a trick. He would never plead for anything, "I don't care."

His hand clutched in her hair. "But I do, Savannah.

I care very much. I care that I hurt you with my thoughtless reaction. I care that my cousin hurt you with his fists.'' He released her hair to brush his hand down the side of her neck to rest against her shoulder. "Do you know what my first thought was when I saw those photos?''

She told herself it didn't matter. Whatever he'd thought, he hadn't *said* enough. She remained stubbornly mute.

He sighed and rubbed his thumb along her collarbone. In a voice husky with emotion, he said, "I thought that if my cousin were alive, I would take pleasure in killing him.''

CHAPTER THIRTEEN

THE deadly intent in Leiandros's voice left no room for doubt in her mind that he meant what he said. Her eyes flew open. "But you—"

He closed her lips with his forefinger. "Shh... I was in shock. You cannot imagine how I felt reading the doctors report and then seeing photos of you bruised and your eyes reflecting every kind of inner devastation."

It was her turn to demand, "Tell me how you felt. Help me imagine it." Had she been wrong to think it was over between them? Did he trust her, but had been too shocked to say so?

His thumb stilled against the beating pulse in her neck. "I was furious, so furious, my mind could not take it in. I felt confused, shaken and somehow at fault. He was my *cousin*."

Her hands slowly unclenched from the quilt to take his hand between them. "Is that why you didn't say anything?"

"Yes." He rubbed her bottom lip with his thumb while turning his other hand to grasp hold of hers with a desperately strong grip.

She felt familiar sensations returning, but she could not give in to them. This was too important. "And now?"

He didn't help, brushing his lips across hers. "If you told me the sky was purple I would believe you."

As declarations went, that was a pretty good one. "Oh," she sighed as his lips touched hers again.

"Will you return to our bed?" he asked, sounding uncertain.

Leiandros sounding anything other than supremely confident was such an anathema, she was incapable of answering for several seconds. He obviously got tired of waiting because he lifted her, quilt, pillow and all. He stood motionless for almost a full minute and she neither moved, nor spoke.

Turning on his heel, he headed for the bedroom.

"I no longer have a choice?" she asked, thinking this behavior fit the man she'd married much better.

He squeezed her against his chest. "I gave you a choice, but you did not protest. You want to return to our bed and I need you to be there, so there you will go."

There was that word again. *Need.* Did he really need her? Even if it was as basic as desire, the prospect that he needed her, Savannah Marie Kiriakis, and no other woman rekindled another spark of the hope she had so recently abandoned.

Linking her hands behind his nape, she pressed her face into the hollow above his shoulder. "There I will go."

He shuddered and hugged her closer.

When they reached the bedroom, he laid her carefully on the bed and removed her bathrobe, his hands moving over her with trembling possessiveness.

"Have you changed your mind about the *no sex* part?"

"No." He glared down at her, his expression so fierce

she had to stifle an urge to roll off the bed and make a run for it. "We make love. It has never been just sex, some animalistic urge that could be satisfied by anyone else."

Oh, Heavens. He shouldn't say things like that. Her throat closed and her eyes filled with tears that seemed easier to shed since Leiandros had held her through the storm after Beatrice's death. She couldn't speak, but he stood their waiting for her acceptance, so she opened her arms and he came into them with gentle force.

They made love so tenderly, she wept from the sheer joy of it afterwards.

Touching her with a soothing motion, he asked, "What happened, *moro mou?*"

She didn't want to look at Leiandros while she told him, so she kept her face pressed against his chest where the beat of his heart soothed her.

"We hadn't had sex since I was four months pregnant with Nyssa and Dion found out she was a girl, too. I didn't mind. It wasn't anything like making love with you. And later, when I found out he had been having affairs all along, I was grateful. I didn't want to risk getting some disease because he felt the need to prove his virility by getting intimate with any woman who would spread her legs for him. Any love I felt for him died during those months."

Leiandros started to speak and then subsided.

"What?" she asked.

"I do not want to interrupt you, but why would he feel the need to prove his virility? He had married an incredibly beautiful woman and fathered two amazing daughters."

Her heart warmed at the compliment and this further proof that Leiandros's view of the world did not match that of his cousin. "I guess he told you all I was pregnant and that's why we had to get married. He was pretty adamant about me getting pregnant immediately anyway. When I didn't, he took me to the doctor for fertility tests."

She remembered the embarrassment she'd felt at that appointment. She didn't speak Greek yet and had no clue what Dion had instructed the doctor to do.

"They came back fine. There was nothing that should stop me from getting pregnant. I was mad at him for making me take the tests, humiliated at what I'd had to go through with a doctor I'd never met to get them done so I insisted he get tested as well. And did I learn to regret that."

Leiandros's hand started rubbing soothing circles against her back.

"His tests came back saying he had a low sperm count. He was devastated and became fixated with proving his manhood. In his mind, impregnating me with a son would do the trick. Our two daughters were like a slap in the face to his thinking *and* I didn't even *conceive* Eva until eleven months into the marriage."

She sighed and snuggled closer to Leiandros's body.

"If I thought going through his monthly temper tantrums when my menses came and being accused of doing everything from having surgery to taking the pill to prevent pregnancy was hard, I had no idea what it would be like when I did fall pregnant. He treated me like a walking incubator and I now realize his affairs started then."

Leiandros made a distressed noise. "And I black-mailed you into trying to have my baby," he said, his voice thick.

She tried to comfort him with her hand against his heart. "I would never have agreed to your demands if I didn't want to fulfill them. I guess I realized somewhere deep in my heart that you truly wouldn't care if the baby was a boy or girl and I wanted your child. I still do," she admitted.

His hand jerked against her back in a hard hug. "Thank you. I don't deserve you." He leaned to kiss the top of her head. "Please tell me about that night."

"I'm leading up to it." She sucked in courage with her next breath to finish the story. She hadn't spoken of it to anyone since the doctor examined her on her return to Atlanta. "He came home one night, pretty drunk, when Nyssa was about six months old. He wanted sex. I said no. He screamed at me, the usual jealous diatribe, condemnation of my character and uselessness as a wife. He called me frigid and host of other names I won't repeat."

Her voice faltered to a halt.

Leiandros filled in the silence. "You said something about not having come to me when you needed me. Was it that night?"

She nodded, her face rubbing against chest. "I was afraid. I sensed that everything was escalating and I didn't know how to stop it. My mind screamed at me to go to you, that you could stop Dion from hurting me or my babies, but I'd gotten so used to stifling the need I felt for you in every way, I stifled that instinct, too."

"He beat you when you refused him sex?" The pain

and fury in Leiandros's voice both soothed her and tugged at her heart.

"No. I told him if he tried to force me, I'd leave Greece. He went out and came home later, this time he wasn't just drunk. He was high on something and terrifyingly not himself. He said more horrible things and started hitting me. I fought back, but I hadn't taken any self-defense classes then. You know, a Southern lady doesn't need them?"

She climbed on top of Leiandros, needing eye contact now when she had shied from it earlier. And she needed to feel her whole body in contact with his while she relived that awful time. "Anyway, he beat me pretty badly and then passed out. I've never been so grateful for anything in my life. You know the rest."

His eyes burned with tender emotion and searing regret. "Yes. I know the rest. You fled Greece and he told the family you hated living there and wanted to return to America. He put on a great show of grieving your loss."

She leaned down to kiss the male flesh that gave her such comfort. "He played the victim very well."

"But in reality you were the victim."

"No," she said fiercely. "I wasn't. I got away, but the rest of his family believed his lies and because of them, they missed out on the first few years of my daughter's lives. They were the real victims."

"*Agapi mou*, you are so generous with your heart, is it any wonder I love you?" He pulled her up until her mouth could meet his and kissed her so tenderly a lump formed in her throat. "*S'agapo*. I love you. *S'agapo*."

That same heart he found so generous wanted to

pound out of her chest. *"You love me?"* she asked with awe and a little disbelief.

"So much. I know you cannot love me now. It will take a long time for you to forgive my blackmail and ruthlessness, if ever, but I can live with that as long as you don't leave me."

Leiandros in a humble mode was almost frightening. She thought about drawing it out, to get a little of her own back for the aforementioned blackmail, but the bleak look in his eyes undermined any such intention.

She tilted her pelvis toward him. "Do you really believe I would have let you touch me after what I went through with Dion, if I had not loved you?"

His flesh stirred against her, but he shook his head. "Perhaps you loved me then, but you cannot love me now. I've mistrusted you, hurt you and failed to protect you from my cousin's cruelty. I do not deserve it, but please promise me you will not leave me. I cannot face a future without you and our daughters."

Tears filled her eyes and spilled over onto her cheeks. "I don't want to leave you, you silly man. *I love you,* Leiandros. I've loved you since that first kiss, but refused to acknowledge it."

He looked at her like he wasn't sure he believed what he had just heard. "You had too much integrity to do so."

She smiled through her tears. "Just as you had too much honor to act on your desire for my body."

"It was more than desire. I fell in love with you that night. Just to be in the same room with you afterward was torture. I had to fight my feelings for six long years. I felt so much guilt I denied my heart and called my love sexual passion. You'll never know the torment I felt when Dion and Petra died in that crash.''

"I know. You lost your baby and your wife.''

He grimaced. "I grieved that, but not as I should have. I grieved the loss of my baby more than Petra and it wasn't even twenty-four hours before my thoughts turned to making you mine. I told myself it was for justice, to replace what I had lost, but the truth is I couldn't live without you anymore. The barriers were gone and so was my self-control.''

She quickly pecked him on the lips for saying such very nice things and then smiled. "So you decided to blackmail me into marrying you.''

He jerked his head in affirmative. "Will you ever be able to forgive me and trust me knowing what a poor husband I was to Petra?''

"You were not a poor husband,'' she admonished him. "If Dion had died and Petra had lived, you would have remained faithful to her and never allowed her to know you loved another woman. I know you, Leiandros. You are too principled to have done otherwise.''

He kissed her with a passion that seemed born of desperation and did not release her mouth until she was limp on top of him.

She smiled dreamily at his gorgeous features. "You have nothing to reproach yourself for.''

His face contorted. "My treatment of you. I believed everything my cousin said about you even though it didn't fit with the woman you had proved to be simply because I felt too guilty to do otherwise. I wanted my cousin's wife with a longing that would not die.''

"I forgive you. I love you. I will *always* love you," she assured him again.

His hands came up to cup her breasts as she leaned back to see his face more clearly. "*S'agapo,* Savannah. I love your spirit and your stubbornness. I love the way you smile when you are happy and hug your daughters when they are tired. I love the way you put up with my mother's craziness before the wedding and acted grateful to do so. But most of all, selfishly, I love your tender heart that can forgive a past wrong and keep loving."

She swallowed down the emotion welling up inside her at his words and gave him a wobbly, misty smile.

He returned the smile, reaching out to tuck a strand of her hair behind her right ear. He let his hand linger to caress the sensitive spot there. "I admire so much the way you reached out to care for an old woman when you were too young to be caring for yourself."

"I was nineteen," she protested.

"A mere babe."

"I'm twenty-seven now, does that make me old enough to take care of myself?" she asked with a saucy look.

His eyes turned grave. "Yes. You are old enough. You are smart enough. You are strong enough, but will you allow me the honor of taking care of you and our family?"

She pressed her breasts into his hot palms. "Yes," she said throatily, "You can take care of me any time you like."

His laughter rumbled up from his chest as he rolled over, pinning her body beneath his. She laughed with him until his movements made her draw her breath and then his mouth covered hers and she was lost.

A few months later, Savannah's Greek doctor, whom Leiandros had taken pains for her to get to know, pronounced her ten weeks pregnant. Ecstatic, she shared the news with Leiandros that night in bed.

Though he was thrilled, he immediately began listing off activities she'd have to curtail for her safety and pronounced she would have to start taking a long nap every afternoon. A nap he sometimes shared with her and provided less sleep than he intended, but Savannah had gotten very adept at getting her way with her Greek tycoon husband.

Eva and Nyssa were over the moon at the prospect of a baby and the grandmothers began fussing over Savannah like two clucking hens.

Six weeks after discovering she was pregnant, Savannah's ultrasound showed twins. They could only determine the sex of one baby, a girl. Leiandros's shell-shocked but obviously joyful response settled Savannah's doubts about his reaction to more daughters once and for all.

After Savannah's second contraction, five months later, Leiandros announced this would be her last pregnancy. He turned an interesting shade of gray as her labor progressed and promised never, ever to do this to her again. Savannah smiled through the pain, knowing the babies would be worth it.

Their third daughter was born first and named Beatrice, shortened almost instantly to Bea by her older sisters. Their son came out squalling and Leiandros came as close to fainting as he ever had in his life when he looked down at the two infinitely precious babies, knowing they were a product of his and Savannah's love. Savannah insisted on naming their son after his father and calling him Leo for short.

Later that day, Savannah lay in the private hospital bed, holding her son while Leiandros sat in a nearby chair and held their new daughter. Eva and Nyssa each perched on a grandmother's knee as Helena and Baptista sat side by side in the window seat.

Leiandros looked up from contemplation of their daughter and met Savannah's gaze. "*S'agapo, yineka mou.* You and our children are my world. My present. My future. My greatest treasure. Gifts from God."

His eyes grew suspiciously moist and his voice choked to a stop while Savannah's eyes sent the same message back to him before she asked if the older girls wanted to sit on the edge of her bed. Soon, they were all engrossed in the babies, the circle of their family complete.

Savannah once again looked deeply into the brown depths of her husband's eyes, eyes that no longer looked enigmatic or mysterious, but blazed with constant love for her and *all* their children.

"Thank you," she said, her heart too full to say any more.

He had promised her she would never be alone again and he had kept that promise, surrounding her with his love, his family and his friends, giving them freely until they became her own.

She would never regret her decision to live her life on the cornerstone of love instead of fear.

Immerse yourself in holiday romance with

BETTY NEELS

Christmas Wishes

Two Christmas stories from the
#1 Harlequin Romance® author.

The joy and magic of this beloved author
will make this volume a classic
to be added to your collection.

Available in retail stores in October 2003.

"Betty Neels pleases her faithful readership with
inviting characters and a gracious love story."
—*Romantic Times*

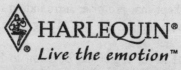

HARLEQUIN®
Live the emotion™

Visit us at www.eHarlequin.com

PHCW

eHARLEQUIN.com

The eHarlequin.com online community is *the* place to share opinions, thoughts and feelings!

- Joining the community is easy, fun and **FREE!**

- Connect with **other romance fans** on our message boards.

- Meet your **favorite authors** without leaving home!

- **Share opinions** on books, movies, celebrities…and *more!*

Here's what our members say:

"I love the friendly and helpful atmosphere filled with support and humor."
—Texanna (eHarlequin.com member)

"Is this the place for me, or what? There is nothing I love more than 'talking' books, especially with fellow readers who are reading the same ones I am."
—Jo Ann (eHarlequin.com member)

**Join today by visiting
www.eHarlequin.com!**

INTCOMM

If you enjoyed what you just read,
then we've got an offer you can't resist!

Take 2 bestselling
love stories FREE!
Plus get a FREE surprise gift!

Clip this page and mail it to Harlequin Reader Service®

IN U.S.A.	IN CANADA
3010 Walden Ave.	P.O. Box 609
P.O. Box 1867	Fort Erie, Ontario
Buffalo, N.Y. 14240-1867	L2A 5X3

YES! Please send me 2 free Harlequin Presents® novels and my free surprise gift. After receiving them, if I don't wish to receive anymore, I can return the shipping statement marked cancel. If I don't cancel, I will receive 6 brand-new novels every month, before they're available in stores! In the U.S.A., bill me at the bargain price of $3.57 plus 25¢ shipping & handling per book and applicable sales tax, if any*. In Canada, bill me at the bargain price of $4.24 plus 25¢ shipping & handling per book and applicable taxes**. That's the complete price and a savings of at least 10% off the cover prices—what a great deal! I understand that accepting the 2 free books and gift places me under no obligation ever to buy any books. I can always return a shipment and cancel at any time. Even if I never buy another book from Harlequin, the 2 free books and gift are mine to keep forever.

106 HDN DNTZ
306 HDN DNT2

Name	(PLEASE PRINT)	
Address	Apt.#	
City	State/Prov.	Zip/Postal Code

* Terms and prices subject to change without notice. Sales tax applicable in N.Y.
** Canadian residents will be charged applicable provincial taxes and GST.
  All orders subject to approval. Offer limited to one per household and not valid to current Harlequin Presents® subscribers.
  ® are registered trademarks of Harlequin Enterprises Limited.

PRES02   ©2001 Harlequin Enterprises Limited

Witchcraft, deceit and more...
all **FREE** from

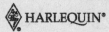

HARLEQUIN®

INTRIGUE®
in October!

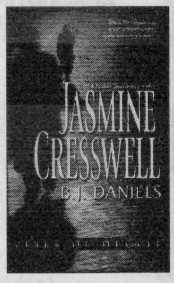

This exclusive offer is valid only in October,
only from the Harlequin Intrigue series!
To receive your **TWO FREE BOOKS** by bestselling romantic
suspense authors **Jayne Ann Krentz** and **Jasmine Cresswell**, send
us 3 proofs of purchase from any 3 Harlequin Intrigue® books sold during the month of October.

*Proofs of purchase can be found in all
October 2003 Harlequin Intrigue books.*

Must be postmarked no later than November 30, 2003.

Visit us at www.tryintrigue.com

HIPOPOC03

The world's bestselling romance series.

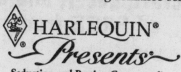

HARLEQUIN®
Presents

Seduction and Passion Guaranteed!

RED HOT REVENGE

There are times in a man's life...
when only seduction will setttle old scores!

Pick up our exciting new series of revenge-filled romances—
they're recommended and red-hot!

Coming soon:

MISTRESS ON LOAN by Sara Craven
On sale August, #2338

THE MARRIAGE DEBT by Daphne Clair
On sale September, #2347

Available wherever Harlequin books are sold.

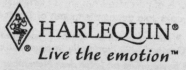

HARLEQUIN®
Live the emotion™

Visit us at www.eHarlequin.com

HPRHR